Khane
A Sci-fi Alien Tail

Holidate With An Alien
RENA MARKS

———◦～◦———

This book is part of the Holidate With an Alien shared world. This Sci-fi Holiday Tail features steamy scenes on an alien world, some heartwarming holidays moments and a guaranteed HEA.

Cover credit: Natasha Snow Designs www.natashasnowde-signs.com

KHANE

"Single, slightly awkward, Earthian female seeking companionship and open-minded individual. Only compatible species may apply. Wealth is appreciated and may move you higher up the list, though not necessary. Looks are necessary, or at least serious muscle tone. Sincere applicants only."

What happens when the daughter of the creator of IDA, the infamous intergalactic dating app, is so socially awkward she can't get past the first date? What if her father gives her a deadline to bring home a suitable match... and it's the holiday party date of the launch of his newest app version?

That's a lot of pressure on one gal to measure up to, so I'm off to beg my gorgeous neighbor, Khane, for help in polishing my dating skills.

One Marjian prince determined to help his neighbor in the compatibility department. One Marjian prince determined to hide his feelings for said neighbor, despite the attempts of his very own bodyguard to push them together. One Marjian prince determined to thwart her matchmaking trials. Because when it comes down to it, he doesn't want anyone else near her.

Revised dating profile by Prince Khane of Marjia: *"Single Earthian female with the beauty of a Goddess seeking an undeserving insignificant male to worship her in the way she deserves to be worshipped. He must be royalty, with a lifelong bodyguard, offer her immeasurable wealth, shower her with love and affection, and be prepared to know that her needs must always come before his."*

There. That should do it.

Pronunciation Guide:
Khane—(Kain)

Tonnie—(TAUN-nie)
Melak'sian—(Ma-LOCK-shun)
Marjian—(Mar-GEE-yun)
Fatija—(Fuh-TEE-huh)

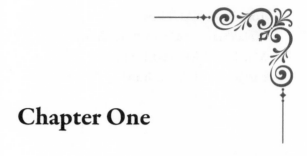

Chapter One

Candace, daughter of Elliot Jameson, Founder of IDA:

"I'm not into sex until I've gotten to know a man."

My date blinks once, and then his expression goes carefully placid. But, best to put that one out there because nowadays, people want to test out their compatibility before getting to know each other. And no matter how fun the night is, why pay for the cow when the milk's free?

Yes, I'm aware I sound like I'm eighty. The last date—I fight the urge to scowl—mentioned it before hightailing it and blocking me from IDA, the Intergalactic Dating App. Sometimes living on a space station sucks, especially when your famous father is involved. My dad is a genius, he created the app, he markets the app, he lives and breathes the app, and the popularity keeps us in the higher circles. It seems that since space travel, dating is awkward no matter how you look at it. Blind dates, dating apps, speed dating, online dating. It's all a vast blur. But it's also necessary for those who live on a space station. There are so many species living here, you almost need the IDA just to know what you're getting.

I wouldn't use it at all if I hadn't gotten myself into a bind. The apartment building in which I live is one of our IDA sponsors. They offered the daughter of the app founder a penthouse apartment in a once in a lifetime deal. I had two years in which to find a match and make my announcement during our latest app version launch, coincidentally, during the Christmas party.

4

This one that I scheduled a date with last night is the pick of the litter. Paul Maraschino, as in cherry—a sexual fruit from old Earth—has thick dark hair that's casually styled, longer on top and shorter on the sides. Blue eyes, a square jaw, and a little cleft in his strong chin. His fingers are long, with clean, square nails. Manly hands, a sprinkling of dark hair on his forearms that disappears into the rolled-up sleeves of his designer shirt.

A Rolex-com on his wrist. His profile pic shows him ruffling the fur of his dog and the sweetness factor makes your ovaries swell.

I can't let this one escape, not after the mound of losers I've had. Maybe I shouldn't have mentioned I wouldn't have sex right away. There's a little voice niggling in my head to flip it around. Not that I can suddenly say I lied, and I am into sex on the first date, but I can work around the original comment. Make it seem less important.

But he beats me to it. "Um, okay, so there's a timeline to follow while we're getting to know each other? And when would that be, Candace? Would we be allowed a kiss on the first date, or would that be cheek only? Air-kisses? What would be the timeline for having sexual relations?"

Does his voice sound the tiniest bit sarcastic?

"I mean, the first date is a no, obviously. We're still strangers," I try to justify. "But if you and I were to have a meaningful connection, and I'm sure we will, the second date might open things up for first base."

First base? I fight the urge to cringe. Where the hell did that phrase pop out from? Pretty sure it came out of my mouth.

"Second date?" My date echoes, seeming stuck on those words and not noticing the first base comment. His eyes are wide, and mouth slightly agape, but no less attractive as the artificial candlelight from the middle of the table glows, lighting and accenting his chiseled features. I can't help but notice he'd like to run, and I start to grow a little desperate because this one is a winner. Not like the last one who lied about his age and produced a pic from fifteen years ago.

I nod, smiling at Paul as seductively as I can. He still hasn't noticed the *first base* comment, which is good. Under the table, I kick off my high heeled shoe so I can use my toes to skim lightly along his shin. Not a creepy, suggestive rub, of course. Just a casual touch with my foot. A connection, one like we might have in bed.

But now he kind of looks like a suffocating fish. His mouth, showing exquisitely capped teeth, opens and closes numerous times. And yet, the bastard still manages to be attractive.

I can't help but sigh dreamily. "I'd be okay with planning the second date now."

Best to let him know one's wants and that we intend to move forward immediately. I'm getting desperate to find a man and I really got lucky with this one.

Silence meets me. And then I take a deep, calming breath.

"So do you come here often?" I ask, and the practiced line is delivered perfectly. My voice is a little bit sultry, a little bit thick, and a little bit sweet, all at once.

"This space station? No!" he practically screams out.

I can't help but wish he had a deeper voice.

My neighbor, Khane has the deepest, sexiest voice I've ever heard. He's here to nurse a broken heart from what Tonnie—his roommate—mentioned.

It makes me sad to think of not living next door to Tonnie and Khane forever. Maybe I can talk Paul into living in my place for as long as possible—at least until we're overrun with children.

I perk up. Maybe Khane and Tonnie would consider buying side by side houses with us once that happens. I'd roll into a ton of money once I'm able to sell my penthouse apartment. Tonnie would make a great uncle of sorts to the little ones.

Paul suddenly looks wary. Maybe right now isn't the best time to ask him about living arrangements.

"So, what brings you to Inap Space Station 8 then? Business?" Dare I hope he traveled this way just to meet me? Because if so, I might forgo my first date rule and the *nickel between my knees*. Another phrase from old Earth, and one that's rather precious to me.

"It's a one-time excursion," he babbles, repeating his earlier thought without answering the question. "I'll never be back. Ever. This is too far east in the Morongulum Galaxy. I can never get another work pass."

I blink. Then why did he come out to meet me? Was he expecting a one-night stand? Or did he figure out that Terrans share surnames and linked mine to my father's? He figured that would give him a leg up in business? It wouldn't be the first time I ran into that.

"And what do you do exactly?"

"Architect. I develop the living structures for space stations or planets that aren't typically livable."

I sigh a breath of relief before the Rolex-com on his wrist flashes a light blue shade.

"If you'll excuse me," he says, "I can't miss this. My mom."

He doesn't wait for my response before tossing his napkin over his half-eaten meal and heading toward the wait rooms.

He tossed his napkin over his plate.

With a sinking sensation, I recognize the red flag. He has no intention of returning.

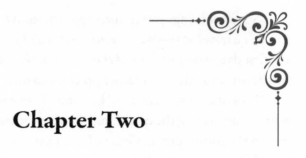

Chapter Two

Khane, Imperial High Prince of Marjia:

"Dry your tears," I growl, feeling powerless at Candace's distress. "The *mierjak* wasn't worth the time."

"I know," she sobs, making me look helplessly over at my body-guard, Tonnie, who also happens to be my brother. "But when will I meet somebody on that damn app who is worth the time? My time is valuable too, you know. I'm not getting any younger."

I fight the snort. She is but a wee *bianca*, an innocent babe in the woods. Or in our case, space. But I know what she means. Her father has given her a deadline in which to bring a suitable date to the launch of the latest version of his dating app. It appears it's a sore point between them that the one person the app can't seem to pair up is his own daughter.

"Have you ever stopped to think that maybe it isn't you?" Tonnie asks. "Maybe it's the app."

Candace gasps like he just called her father's precious app the garbage of the universe.

I glare at my brother, and he shrugs sheepishly.

"I'm sure your father did a wonderful job with the app," I say trying to smooth things over. "But on our planet, we don't meet others via a match service. Ever."

"His app is state of the line—"

I can't help but zone out at the rest of her words. I've heard it all before.

His app determines the ultimate matching between species.

It's not based on looks.

It's not based on status.

It's not based on wealth.

His app is state of the art—based on compatibility.

"Yes, but the app is only as good as the information you enter," I say when she finally stops speaking.

"I know," she wails. "That's why Tonnie wrote my bio for me. And it worked to get me dates, I just can't get past the first one. I'm socially inept. Awkward when spoken to. Generally, emotionally stunted."

Socially inept? She should try living on my planet, where a male and his bodyguard must agree on who might be the next queen. There's no shortage of scheming females in line to the throne. Hell, the last one claimed to be royalty, like me, but broke the imperial rule of virginity. I'd burst into her waiting room to find her being plowed by her own bodyguard. Thankfully, there was no affiliation between them.

I don't mention that I had a tip and it was the perfect out to a relationship I no longer wanted.

"That's not what I mean. Look, my species, a Marjian Fenal, might be compatible with a Lastrosard." I wave in the general vicinity of our neighbor, who is one. "But I'll never know if I don't enter my own data correctly in the app."

"There are fail safes for that. Maybe you enter that you're not compatible with a Lastrosard, but Tonnie also enters, and he may say that he is. Ten other Marjians may enter and say that they are, so now the app researches couples to see if the compatibility between the two has been verified and determines your original data was incorrect."

I'll need to present this a different way. "I'll give you that. Then how many Marjians are in your app?"

Candace flips out her com and brings up the app. "None," she says flatly. "Wait, that can't be right." She presses some more buttons.

"Here's something. A Marj*sian*. It could be a misspelling. Or a completely different species. Don't you sometimes refer to yourselves as Marjians instead of Marjian Fenals? What if someone enters a Fenal? Or if they're too lazy and calls themselves a Mar Fenal? Oh, my gosh, that's in there too."

"My point exactly. My people don't use a dating app so maybe someone entered what they thought about us and spelled it wrong. And I'm sure there are countless other species here on this space station that don't use a dating app. You know why?"

She shrugs. "Why?"

"Because dating apps are for losers."

Tonnie grimaces and I scowl, already aware it wasn't the smoothest line, but this isn't the first time she's been distressed over meeting a loser on the app. I'm frustrated that she continues to waste time on it. "I mean, let's pretend that ninety-five percent of males who get on to that app aren't looking for a mate or a companion or a date. They're just saying they are. Now suppose that ninety-five percent of females are looking for a relationship. That leaves a lot of trusting females who are disappointed, all looking for that last five percent of males who aren't lying about what they want."

"I see," she says slowly, and I notice her tears have dried. "So do you think that I need to keep dating?"

"Exactly," Tonnie says. "And stop taking it to heart when you're disappointed. Remember, the majority of males on this app are losers."

"But what if it's not them?" Candace says. "What if it's me? This last one seemed perfectly normal until I ruined things."

"It's not you," I growl. How can she even think that? She is wonderful, adorably witty, fun to be around, she smells of flowers.

"What was it that you'd said right before this last one shut down?" Tonnie asks.

"Paul the Prick," I growl out.

Candace nods in agreement over the name that I amended.

"I think it was when I mentioned that I don't have sex on the first date," she says defensively.

Tonnie bursts out laughing.

I glare at him, and he makes an effort to stifle it behind his hand.

"Nothing wrong with that," I say, patting her on the shoulder. I can't help but notice how slender it seems without the massive muscles of our species. I rather like how soft she is. "You keep stating what you want. I think subconsciously you were starting to realize that a lot of these males were after one thing."

"Yeah," she says. "You're right. I should trust my instincts. You're so smart."

I preen a little.

"Here's a new idea," Tonnie says. "Why don't you let Khane pick your next date?"

Something twists inside my gut. I find the idea abhorrent. I'm about to refuse when Candace looks up at me with bright eyes.

"Would you, Khane? Pretty please? I would love your help. You're so together all the time. I can't imagine you having dating issues."

No, never. They line up to kiss my crown. And it's not what I want.

But I'm lost in the depths of those pretty violet eyes. I can't resist her request. And I scowl at Tonnie's chuckle because the fool knows it.

"Of course, *inca*. You know I will."

She hands me her com with the app still open and I can't help but admire her profile pic. She's a beautiful female, despite being so small; no wonder she gets so many losers. They're determined to own this beauty.

I flip through the first request.

"Oh, I thought that one had promise..." her voice trails off as I flip through the second and third.

"Look, he owns his own home..."

I flip through that one.

"Okay, are you at least going to tell me what I'm missing here?"

I quickly flip through the next several.

"If a male needs to prove to you he owns a home, he's dangling a carrot," Tonnie says. "Chances are it's not even his."

"Oh."

"Same thing if they take a picture with a pet. A relative's *bianca*. Or even their sister," I mutter.

I flip through the loser who had pictured himself with his grand-sire.

Then I look up, exasperated. "Are all of these idiots human?"

"I-uh, I have my app set for human only," she stammers. "It was simpler since I don't have to research each species before the date." Her cheeks are pink as if she's ashamed to admit she's making it easier for herself.

But my heart races because obviously she's not into it. If she was, she'd want to learn all about the person's race, their culture, their interests. Even their language. Just as I paid an ungodly amount of money for downloads for one called French.

"Pfft. Just enter Terran and Marjian, then," Tonnie says. "You know those two species well."

She nods. "If there were any of your species in there, I certainly would," she agrees.

She misses that we had the conversation that my kind would never go onto such a worthless app. Still, I understand that she thinks her father's app has value.

As ugly as the males are with their round, balding heads, and lack of majestic horns.

"You seem to be enthralled with humans from Earth," I growl accusingly.

She stammers. "Ah-I, well, it would be nice to live planet bound instead of on a space station."

Tonnie's grin grows wider. I detest living on a space station also, and he knows it. The only reason why we're still here is because she needs us. Otherwise, I'd have returned home long ago.

"Your date from last night was a traveler," I point out, fighting the snarl in my voice.

"I got a little desperate. Figured I made my bed, now I need to lay in it."

Tonnie chuckles again. He is enamored with Candace and her quirky sayings. He thinks she will be perfect for me. I'm not sure why. She's outrageous and realistic, not self-absorbed at all—completely opposite the princess I was engaged to last year before he and I decided to take time away from the planet to heal from the scandalous breakup. But Candace is unique, quoting her old-fashioned quips as if they make sense to everyone. I've teased her many times just to be introduced to a new one as if they're common knowledge.

"Oh, wait," she says as I flip through the two-hundredth loser. "That one speaks French."

"French? That old language?" I ask, like I haven't studied it myself. My eyes narrow as I flip back to the previous fool. I snort at the oiled bush he grows over his upper lip.

"Isn't that one of the languages you studied on the last space station?" Tonnie asks. "For fun?" He turns to her. "Khane is a master at learning languages, you know."

"It is," I say quickly, trying to stop him from sharing more information. I'd learned the stupid Earthian language because she'd mentioned once before that if she ever visited Earth, she'd love to see France. And I wish Tonnie didn't know. He finds it amusing to mention and hope she'll ask questions like how long I've known it and how I could learn it in such a short amount of time. Which might lead to: *How much did you pay to have it downloaded?* All of that leads to the question of why.

A new idea pops into my head. If I have to watch her flirt with a loser, I may as well let her see every human male on this app is an idiot.

"It's the language of love," Candace says, and her eyes sparkle.

Love? An image of Candace entwined with this moron enters my imagination. I feel my horns grow hot and my *stremma* emerge.

"Oh, what's happening?" she asks, her eyes wide on my bare chest.

"Nothing," I growl, aware of the stripes of color changing my skin tone to red and white. I refuse to look at Tonnie. "Just hot in here."

"Do you all change color?" Candace asks, looking at Tonnie.

He nods. "It is the same as when you blush." He tweaks her nose. "A pretty pink."

And it's not exactly when we're hot with temperature. It's more like a tell-tale sign of a heated emotion, jealousy, anger—or arousal—and if he tells her, he'll find my fist in his face, bodyguard or no.

"My colors are different than Khane's," Tonnie says. "Purple and white."

"Red's my favorite color," Candace says and damn if pleasure doesn't hit me, making the *stremma* disappear completely. Is she aware that my shades are her favorite? "I love the holidays on Earth. Our colors are red and green."

"Together?" Tonnie sounds aghast.

She laughs instead of taking offense. "We use the brightest, most colorful shades that time of year."

"Huh," Tonnie says. "Sounds like All Halle Syence. We dress up one night in obnoxious shades for the *biancas* and pass out sweet meats. Parents hate it, meat should be savory, not sweet."

"Oooh, I'd like that too," Candace says. "We give out presents."

"Anyway," I interrupt. "I messaged this Brian Goodyear of Earth. He's on Inap 8 for about three sun-cycles."

Which is perfect because if he charms her, he'll be heading to his own planet without the two getting to know each other. Long distance relationships never work out.

Instead of handing her com back, I lift her arm. Her skin is soft and smooth beneath my touch, and I flip it over to attach her bracelet.

Gooseflesh breaks out along her arm, and I like that. I like that I affect her.

I'm an idiot.

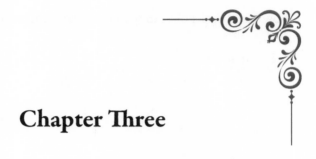

Chapter Three

Candace:

Date number two. I have good vibes about this one, I do. Mostly because it was Khane who picked him, and I have the utmost respect for Khane's opinion.

And Khane's remarkably ridged abs, which I've seen many times we've lounged at the pool. The last time however... seeing him up close, with that powerful body and his stormy gaze, sent shivers of awareness running down my spine. My breath had caught, and I was barely aware that he'd asked me something because I was so focused on him. Had his horns always been so majestic? Such a beautiful silvery-white? His features so sculpted? His cheekbones so sharp? He looks like an old-fashioned Prince Charming with his black and silver-chunked, streaked hair.

"How long have you lived on this space station?" Brian Goodyear of Old Earth asks, sitting across from me, tearing me from my Khane-daydream. His nose is wrinkled like he can't stand the thought of living here within the confines of the dome, breathing the recycled, purified air and not having to suffer from wild bouts of weather.

"Three years," I respond cheerily, much more relaxed than I was on the last date.

He's not as wealthy as Paul was; no Rolex sits on Brian's wrist. But then again, if his name means what I think it does, his family business probably slid downhill about the time vehicles became obsolete in favor of the hovercraft a couple decades ago. I mean, rubber tires aren't exactly a booming demand anymore.

"Seems like a great place."

"It is. I love it. Everyone is incredible, very supportive of other species and cultures. It's such a wide array of people, I imagine it would be a great place to raise a family. To teach your children about diversity."

There. Seed number one planted.

But Brian shudders. "Kids."

I lean forward. "You don't like them?"

"Not other people's. I imagine someday I'd like my own."

I settle back into my chair. Okay. I can live with that. It wasn't a hard no to a family.

"Does Earth still have various accents?" I ask suddenly. "You mentioned you speak other languages?"

He blinks behind his glasses, a bit owlishly. Maybe his eyes are the tiniest bit magnified by the lenses? It probably shouldn't turn me off.

I've seen Khane in glasses. He doesn't use them regularly, just when he's out in the dome. Domes are provided to filter the harsh rays of planet's suns, but sometimes the domes blur distance for a lot of species. So, with glasses, he looks more like a professor. With horns. A sexy horned professor with amazing abs that he shows off a lot. As well he should. He's not a braggart, he's simply comfortable around me; we're at the temperature-controlled pool most days.

Come to think of it, lots of times when we're in our apartments, he's also shirtless. While Tonnie smirks like he's aware of something and Khane scowls like Tonnie's holding it over his head.

Huh. I'll have to pay attention to the smirking next time.

I pick up my glass of wine and take a gulp. Maybe if I can blur my vision just a little bit, I won't notice Brian's large eyeballs.

"Um, yes? The Brits still talk funny." He smiles, and maybe his front teeth are a smidge too large. "Those in the Americas talk pretty normally, though."

I snort. He must be from the Americas. "France? Italy? Spain?"

He blinks and again, the great horned owl comes to mind. "Well, yes."

I try to look sweet and unassuming, but did he forget his profile said he spoke the language of love?

"Do you think you can show me? It's been so long since I've watched an Earth vid," I say. "I can barely remember what an accent sounds like."

He clears his throat. I can't help but think that's a bit rude for the table. I cover my lips with my napkin, hoping he'll get the hint.

"*Je rêve de tremper ma baguette dans ta soupe.*"

He waits for my reaction, preening a bit. I have no idea what he said.

"I, uh, I didn't realize you spoke French," I say. "I thought you were just going to say something in Universal and use a French accent." I have to admit, I'm impressed. Most people wouldn't bother, not for a language used nowhere but old Earth.

"I would have," he says. "But when second languages come easily to some, I couldn't resist showing my skill."

Oh. Well, that's impressive, in a cocky way.

"What did it mean?" I ask.

"I'd love to know if your skin is as soft as it looks." Brian looks deeply into my eyes, takes my hand, and skitters his thumb along the sensitive skin at the top.

I'd love to give in to feelings and emotions... but I'm stuck wondering why the French words for *skin* and *soft* sound remarkably similar to *bread* and *soup*. That much anyone knows. We're sitting in a restaurant right now. Hell, there's a baguette with soup on the menu.

"Maybe you can say something in our language and just use the accent?" I prod.

He sighs. "I'll try but it's not easy to turn off the knowledge in my mind." He taps the side of his head.

"*Bellisima, cara amia, c'est sûr que tu n'es pas la fille la plus jolie ici, mais j'éteindrai la lumière.*" He shakes his head self-deprecatingly. "Apologies. I did it again. Too much learning in my head."

Ugh, he does the throat clearing thing again. A spike of irritation sparks at the base of my neck. Is this a recent habit and will it run its course?

"Candace Jameson, ma cherie, your eyes bring a man to his knees." His accent rolls but it's unused, a little rickety, and not quite... what I need. Maybe he just needs practice... I can overlook this—

"Odd that your interpretation doesn't match your words, considering you had told my friend that she's obviously not the loveliest lass in the sea, but you'd be willing to turn out the lights."

I startle at the deep rumble that comes from behind me. That's the accent that does it for me. The depth, the richness of the sexy baritone voice. Again, I seem to be comparing Khane to a more limited human—

And why does everything remind me of Khane suddenly? I even imagine the sound of his voice. But then the meaning of the comment hits me.

"Wait, what?" I turn around to see it is indeed Khane, here in the restaurant, checking up on us.

He's bristling with anger, the faint red and white stripes of his *stremma* showing on his arms, neck, and face—all exposed skin. And... that's kind of sexy because I know how those stripes look on his ripped chest.

"Where did you learn your language?" Khane snarls at Brian. "Because you just insulted one of my best friends."

Does he mean me? Is he calling me one of his best friends? I can't help the soft smile as I take him in, standing majestic and proud with his horns polished and his back stiff. He's wearing a scowl on his face, and it makes me smile because he's insulted for me.

"Brian, meet Khane. He's my neighbor... and best friend," I say. I guess, I mean, I hadn't noticed until he mentioned it, but he is the one I come to with all my secrets. My hopes. My dreams.

Brian's watching my face, then leans back and considers. "Well, that's strange, don't you think? A human female and male alien who are best friends?"

"Strange?" Khane snarls.

And what does he mean by male alien? Why wouldn't the humans be the aliens?

Brian straightens his spine. "I was being nice because ladies are present. I meant it was inappropriate."

"Inappropriate?" I gasp. I can't believe what he's saying. "What do you mean?"

He leans forward and gives me a look that my father might. "I mean, no man would want his girlfriend to be best friends with another man. Even if he is just an alien."

I suck in a whoosh of air, which makes my bosom swell to inappropriate points, makes Brian do a double take... and makes Khane's *stremma* glow brightly. No mistaking his colors now.

Khane:

"So, the male pretended to know French on his bio?" Tonnie's eyebrows shoot up to his hairline.

I shrug. "Apparently. He must've studied a few basic phrases suitably impressive to use during dining."

"I never want to hear that language again!" Candace snarls. "A *speciesist*, to boot."

"I don't blame you, *inca*," Tonnie says soothingly. "We should find you another favorite language from your planet."

I give him a look. It took me a good three months of consistent downloads to learn the last one because of his idiot idea that it would make our human neighbor feel more at home.

"Italian. That's a romantic language, also, isn't it, pet?" Tonnie asks, smoothing the hair that rolls over her shoulder.

"Yes," she says thoughtfully. "That shall be my newest favorite language. No more French. Ever."

"So, what happened after you asked him to leave?"

"He stomped off like he was the injured party," Candace sniffs. "Then the human server came around with the check to say it was paid and that *my brother* left his number scrawled on it for her to call him."

Tonnie sucks his breath in.

"Even worse? He didn't pay it out of the goodness of his heart. It was in the IDA contract that he had to pay, no matter what. I added that request in after the last loser." She looks rather proud of herself.

"Then what happened?" Tonnie asks.

"Khane sat down to enjoy dessert."

Tonnie barks a laugh.

I shrug. "Ordered six more to go. Everything on the menu. His credit line was already on file. Told the server Candace's brother wouldn't mind and she should thank him during their date."

Candace giggles and it lights my heart. We'd walked to a pond afterward, sat down on the bench, spread out the desserts between us and shared a fork to taste every single one of them.

What happened next was mind boggling.

"Oh, Khane. This one is the bomb." She'd moaned—literally moaned like a female would while being licked within an inch of her life—and closed her eyes as she tossed her head back, exposing the slender line of her neck, the pulse throbbing as it taunted me.

Tafanyak. A sinful thought sneaked into my mind—the taste of the dessert on her lips.

"Chocolate and cherries. The sweet and sour, the texture. Probably shouldn't have started with this one because surely nothing else can live up."

I'd grunted, hoping the sound would inhibit the growing bulge below my belt. "Males probably wouldn't find it as delectable as females."

Her gorgeous violet eyes snapped open. "How much you want to bet?"

From what I understand, Terrans from Earth have basic eyes. Brown, blue, green, and similar shades in-between. Those who've been exposed to constant traveling to space portals, including the chemical cleansing of DNA for each one, have found their eye color becoming more clarified.

Hence Candace's stunning violet eyes. Gorgeous, beautiful eyes.

I narrowed mine. "What do you have?"

And because I was still sporting a stiff rod between my legs, I couldn't help but peer down her neckline.

She'd smacked my chest, leaving a warm imprint of her palm. I fought the urge to grab her hand and press it to my bare skin.

"So bad!" she'd laughed. "Yes, I have boobies. Two of them, unfortunately. I know your species prefers three."

"I can make do with two."

She raised her brows. "You are such a man! Here, taste this. The way to a man's heart is his stomach, you know." She held up her fork with a new dessert sample on it.

I'd chuckled. My best friend cracks me up with her old-fashioned phrases. I ran across her idiosyncrasies when I studied her old Earth language, French. I had access to looking up all the outlandish things she says.

She's fascinating. How she remembers them all, I'll never know.

I leaned in to take a bite, but she waved the fork slightly to the side and giggled.

"Feed me, you selfish female," I'd growled at her teasing. "No wonder you're having a hard time attracting decent males."

She laughed again, knowing I tease because all she's had are losers not worthy of her time. It isn't her fault humans don't deserve an ultimate goddess like her.

When she'd lifted the fork back up to my lips, we both froze. All laughter died away as we gazed into each other's eyes, aware of a tension filled moment between us. Fighting the moment, I leaned forward to take the bite she offered.

And groaned when I got a glimpse of the sweet, delectable curves beneath her neckline.

Fortunately, her eyes were glued to my lips as I bit into the dessert and didn't notice my indiscretion.

"Delicious?" she'd asked, her voice husky as she watched my jaw work.

"Delectable. You were right."

"But we have six others to try before we can decide which is the best."

"You're right. We should get moving on that." I took the fork from her hand, hyper-aware of the brush of our fingers meeting, and take a piece of the next dessert before holding it up to her mouth.

She opened eagerly.

This time a growl rumbled from my chest when my imagination hit, and I thought about her lips wrapped around my cock instead of the fork.

But Candace wants a human. She's made that abundantly clear by setting her app parameters. By the numerous tales she tells us of old

Earth. By mentioning how much she'd prefer to live on the planet yet is unable to because her father travels from space station to space station. Her race, New Terran, is dependent upon parents until they marry. It is an archaic custom, but who am I to interfere with her traditions. I, who have not been without my bodyguard since birth.

"You have a little sauce right here," she'd said, swiping her finger at the corner of my lip. Instead of wiping off her finger, she sucked it clean.

A whoosh of desire tingled down my spine.

"Thank you," I'd said, fighting the growl that threatened my speech, and picked up a berry from a slice of cake to press to her lips. She opened her mouth, and her tongue touched my finger, nearly making me groan. My mind was flying high, wondering at all these thoughts and feelings and urges between us. We ate every single dessert and then, complaining about sugar overload, we lay down on the soft carpet of grass-like plant which covered the park, and stared up at the stars. Somehow my arm ended up underneath her neck, letting her use me as a pillow, and maybe we would never have thought anything about it. But now with this tension brimming between us I was hyper aware of the weight of her head, the scent of her hair, the sweet profile of her strange alien face as she gazed up at the night sky.

"So, when's your next date?" Tonnie asks. The memories I'd been recalling burst like dancing bubbles as I'm yanked back to the present.

"I'm not sure." Candace taps her fingertips against the table thoughtfully. "I have a dinner party with my father this weekend. I'll be staying at the Emursi resort, I guess while I'm there I can scroll the app for possible dates during the evening next week." She winces. "Of course, my father was expecting me to bring one of my dates since I kind of led him to believe Paul was a winner. And when things fell through with Paul, I was sure Brian was going to pull through." She sighs. "I guess now I'll be going alone and fielding off their suggestions on how to use the app, as if I don't know how, and listen to their concerns about how I need to make sure I find a date for the holiday party per my residential contract." She turns to me. "That's the launch, you know. He wants to reveal the new version of the app right before Christmas so that people would want to buy it as gifts for friends. It's a huge time of year for purchases."

"We'll find you someone by then," I assure her and ignore Tonnie's pointed look. "How hard can it be? Even though you're missing a few body parts?" I hold up her hand to mine, then entwine our fingers, showing her that my last two are missing one of hers to come between them.

And the area below my belt remembers that she's missing the third breast. No matter, I'll mash the two she's got together and lick the two nipples back and forth.

She sighs again but doesn't let go of my hand. And I shouldn't find that I feel like an inexperienced young male on his first date, but I do. "Wish I could get out of going to this party. It's the last one before the release though, so there's no way. It'll just be me and a bunch of app fanatics talking statistics."

"*Appies*!" Tonnie says.

Candace looks blank and I have to explain the idiot's meaning. "Like Trekkies."

"You guys watch Star Trek?"

"Oh, Khane loves the classics. Your planet knew about other life forms back then when the series was released, you know," Tonnie says, ignoring my snarl. "It was covered up by your government for decades."

"I'd rather have a Trekkie than an Appie," she says glumly.

Tonnie's grin is bright. "Khane, go pull up your favorite episode. I'll make some popcorn."

I can't believe he just let out my secret fetish. But then Candace leans in.

"I love Star Trek," she whispers conspiratorially and suddenly I'm glad.

"Then sit next to me, *inca*. I'm afraid Tonnie will sway you with his sarcastic cracks."

The muscles in my thigh tighten when she does just that, scooting up against me so our legs touch.

Then I catch my breath when she lifts my arm and lays it across her shoulders.

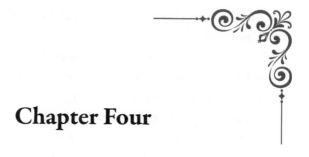

Chapter Four

Candace:

The Emursi resort is fit for royalty with its two-story tall ceilings and floors polished like glass.

The massive hotel is boldly overstated, featuring fixtures of gold which symbolizes wealth back when the metal was precious, and deep purple velvet fabrics reminiscent of the royals of many cultures.

Father had taken one look at me, and his winged eyebrow rose as his assistant ushered me to my room where a delicate gown of iridescent pink waited. It was cinched tight at the waist with a purple belt, the same shade of purple that matched my father's tie.

Of course, he would want his only daughter marked as a member of the Jameson family, despite what a disappointment I've been. Even now, I sit awkwardly at a table as Father and his assistant, Amelia, flit around, knowing exactly what to say to garner interest in his cause.

Me? I can't even use the app to find a suitable date, much less talk it up with technical issues.

I wish Khane—and Tonnie—were here. I'd have someone to talk to and quite frankly, I'm a different person around them. I'm more social, not as reserved, definitely not as awkward. I'm not sure what it is but I've never felt like an outsider around those two. They truly are my best friends.

There's a warm glow in my chest knowing that I have best friends. First time ever. Traveling your whole life from space station to space station didn't allow a lot of friendships to form. But now? I have two. So worth the wait.

I'm barely aware of one of the resort staff tapping my father's shoulder and whispering into his ear. What catches my awareness is the way he grows excited, his eyes brightening and his spine straightening as he brushes imaginary dust from his shoulder and responds to the staff.

Then he uses a gold spoon—ironic, because isn't the phrase *born with a silver spoon*—to tap the elegant crystal stemware he holds.

A sound that makes me cringe as I imagine the delicate glass shattering with his exuberant ringing.

"Your attention, please. May I have your attention?"

The chatter in the room grows quiet.

"Thank you. I'm extremely excited—and honored—to present two people interested in IDA from"—his voice grows reverent— "the Marjian Fenal district."

Gasps roll around the room and I'm utterly confused. Quickly I recall the conversation with Khane and Tonnie about how their species doesn't use any type of dating apps—is that the reason for the excitement over these two joining us?

But then my confusion evaporates as the double doors open and Khane and Tonnie stand in the doorway.

Father rushes up to them, his hand held out to greet them.

Tonnie steps forward first, vetting father's exuberant introduction as Khane's eyes search the room—and land on me.

I can't believe this. I can't believe they came here to support me. Slowly I stand as Father's voice rings out, making introductions while clapping fills the air. But all of that noise drowns out as Khane marches toward me.

He stops right before me, holds out his hand and I find myself slipping mine into his.

He bows, like an old-fashioned, stately prince, and kisses it. All eyes are on us, and I feel my cheeks bloom with pink.

"You came," I whisper.

"We couldn't let you face all of this by yourself," he says. "Besides, who would be here to help you pick your next date?"

And with that, my excitement plummets because the idea of Prince Charming vanishes before my eyes.

Khane:

I watch as the expression freezes on her beautiful face. Something that I said caused her pain that she's trying not to show.

"Candace. You didn't tell me you knew anyone from planet Marjia, much less Khane, the Imper—"

"Your daughter is my neighbor," I cut in, not sure if his announcement was about to reveal my status. The last thing I need is people swarming us. "And my best friend," I utter, wanting to bring that spark of happiness back to her. This female is too beautiful to ever be unhappy.

It works. Her expression softens.

"Well," her father says, surprise evident in his voice. "It's nice to know that with all her evenings spent on her couch, she had time to do some socializing..."

"Her evenings are spent on my couch. Our couch," I amend, adding Tonnie to the conversation.

Immediately he knows what I'm doing. "Yes, yes," Tonnie says to Elliot Jameson. "Candace is always at our place or we're at hers. Sometimes we congregate at the pool or meet for dinners at the restaurant in the lobby."

"Still best friends then?" she whispers for my ears only.

"Always." I hold out my pinky toward her, aware that my sixth finger is an extra compared to hers. She'd giggled when she discovered it, back when she was teaching me to pinky swear.

She intertwines her much smaller pinky with mine, completing the swear.

"Room at your table for two more?" I ask before we drop hands.

"Of course," she says. "A seat on either side of me."

"We shall squeeze a seat in between Candace and me," her father interjects, letting everyone know he eavesdrops.

I nod my head. I'm aware of what he's implying, that I'll be the one to sit next to him while he tries to entice me to promote his baby, the IDA. He has no idea it'll be Tonnie sitting there while I take the seat on the other side of Candace.

Just then, familiar music begins to pipe through the meeting room.

"The Marjian anthem," I say.

Her father beams. Obviously, he ordered the song for Tonnie and me.

Tonnie holds up his hand to Elliot. "It is my duty to dance with an honored female for the first playing of our anthem," he says.

Technically, as my guard he is supposed to vet the females intended for me, a time-honored tradition.

"Please keep with your conversation," I say, waving my hand toward her father. "I will take Candace to dance." I hold my hand out for her, and she takes it without hesitation. I immediately sweep her away to the dance floor.

"Wow, everyone's staring," she whispers as I hold her close. Her gorgeous eyes flit around the room.

I cock my head. "Surely you realize you are a beautiful female."

She blinks, those gorgeous violet eyes staring up at me. "Oh no. I'm just passable. No more so than anyone else."

"Oh, you're wrong. You have inner beauty and pure beauty without artifice. Any male would be lucky to have you. Unfortunately, you are only attracting males who are interested in your father's position and what you can do for them." I let that sink in for a moment and then gently swirl her out.

When I bring her back to me, she says, "I think it's *you* that people are enamored with."

"I'm sure they're curious about my reclusive species."

"Oh yes," she says dryly. "I'm sure all these women are interested in your species as a whole."

I growl softly at her but can't hold the grin from my lips. After the song ends, I take pity on Tonnie who has been fending off her father all this time. "Do you mind dancing with Tonnie so he can take a break from discussing your app?"

"Poor Tonnie. Of course not."

I wave him over and almost feel bad at the look of relief he gives me. I lean forward and press a soft kiss to Candace's forehead before I warn him. "Just one. Don't leave me alone with him too long."

"Suck it up," Tonnie growls. "I was there for two songs. Two. Whole. Songs."

He whisks her away, leaving me to bite back a grin while I head to where Elliot Jameson stands. I hope to distract him from what he considers Candace's downfalls by letting him try to entice me into supporting his app.

"Your bodyguard doesn't think he'd be interested in entering a bio for the dating program," Elliot says. "But how about you? It would be most beneficial to have someone of your stature enter the server right before our launch."

"I'll have to give it some thought."

He leans in, hoping to hook me. "Even if you're not looking for something long term, the app could help you find a suitable date just for the party. Plus, it'll give us immeasurable data."

I smile thinly. "I already know all of this from your daughter. If anyone can get me or Tonnie to sign up it will be her."

"Oh, but Candace isn't trained on selling the app. I've allowed my daughter quite a bit of leeway—freedom to go her own way—when it comes to the company."

"Yet you've given her an ultimatum for this launch date?" I raise my eyebrows, letting him know that I'm aware of why her presence is in the app. He flushes a dark red, a color that's similar to my *stremma*.

And like triggers like because I look away quickly as I feel the familiar tingle begin at the base of my spine. I fight the sensation down. I don't need people wondering what our changing colors mean, or adding that detail to their app and finding out it marks the royal line.

"Not my doing, unfortunately. Candace entered a contract for that plush apartment through one of our sponsors. She had three years to find an IDA supported match or she defaults on the loan."

That's interesting. She's not tied to Inap 8 then.

When the dance ends and Tonnie brings Candace back. Her eyes are bright and sparkling, her cheeks are flushed. She's never looked more beautiful. And when it's time to be seated for dinner, Tonnie takes Candace to the table, pulling out her chair for her to sit. I stay back further, in line with her father. When her father turns to his assistant right before sitting in his own chair, Tonnie and I perform a smooth maneuver, crossing each other as Tonnie takes the chair to Candace's left and I take the empty chair at her right.

"Well, hello, beautiful," I say smirking at her as I sit in the chair.

"Slick," she utters with the sly grin, letting me know she's aware of Tonnie getting stuck with her father. "But you're so gonna owe Tonnie."

I wince. "He's rather dramatic. He'll never let me live this down."

From her left, Tonnie mutters loudly enough for us to hear, "You got that right."

Candace giggles as our plates are brought out. When we're nearly done with our meal she asks, "Did you guys book a room here? The views are incredible."

"No, they're completely sold out. The conference had been booked for a while. We'll have to head home afterward."

She gasps. "That's an hour flight. I have a suite, Khane. You'll both stay with me. After all we're going to the same place in the morning. We can all catch a flight together."

"How big is your suite?" Tonnie whispers from her other side. He makes sure her father's attention is turned toward his assistant.

"It has living quarters with a functional extra bed, a kitchenette, and a separate bedroom. I can give you guys the larger bedroom, and I'll take the sofa bed in the living room."

"I'm not sleeping with him," Tonnie growls.

"It's your suite," I remind Candace, ignoring Tonnie. "You take the bedroom, and we'll figure it out."

She looks like she wants to argue but her father turns his attention back to Tonnie.

"Sir Tonnie, may I introduce my assistant, Amelia? I would be lost without her expertise..."

Whatever other babble he's about to utter fades away as I focus on Candace.

"Your dress is gorgeous. It's a good color on you."

"Thank you. Pinks and reds look good against my skin."

A flash of heat swells in my groin at the image of me wrapped around her with the matching shades of my *stremma* emerged.

Curiously, Elliot Jameson sits back, content. His assistant is chatting up Tonnie, working hard to get him to agree to enter the program, and both lean toward each other over Elliot Jameson. My focus is on Candace.

I hear Tonnie bark out laughter and I turn to see him with his head close to Amelia. She's showing Tonnie the details of the app. Elliot Jameson has moved himself over to Amelia's seat when a slight ping goes off on Candace's phone.

"They're getting along rather well," Candace whispers. "Is that a good thing? I like Amelia. But she does work for my dad."

Then her father speaks loudly. "Oh, good. That's the data I had Amelia enter on someone who I think might very well be a suitable match for you, Candace. He's in town for a few days so I'd like you to meet him. He's a rising young entrepreneur and shows amazing promise."

Candace's face falls.

Her father turns to me. "I have amazing intuition for young people and their work ethic. After all, I found Amelia." He winks. "And Candace is still required to make a suitable match to announce at the Christmas Ball." He rubs his hands together. "The launch of the new app."

From behind him, his assistant looks miserable. I see her mouth to Candace, "I'm sorry."

Chapter Five

Candace:

By the end of the night, Tonnie's had a bit more drink than he's used to. Apparently, wine spritzers for Marjians are the equivalent of tequila for humans.

Father has long since retired to his room and it's just me and Khane, Tonnie, and Amelia. To her credit, she's still on the clock, working hard to show him the benefits of joining the app. In response, Tonnie's taunting her, his voice low and flirty, telling her how he met her in person and not through an app.

Khane's eyebrows shoot to his hairline. Pretty sure he notices the same thing I do... that Amelia must've been flirting back with Tonnie earlier for him to continue it in front of us. To be fair, Khane and I were focused on each other mostly. He'd mentioned to have this upcoming date at the restaurant in our apartment building where he could sit at the bar and be on standby in case I needed him.

I don't intend to need him. I can't have him join the mentality of everyone else and think that Candace can't keep a date to save her soul, even when her father makes a perfectly good choice for her. I have no qualms that my father's choice isn't flawless—if this fails, it's all me.

I'm determined to make this date work, come hell or high water. If he has a great big wart on his nose, I'll grin and bear it. And try not to get stuck staring at it, drawn like a moth to a flame.

If he's poor as a church mouse, I'll assure him that's not a problem. Even if he's getting to know me just to get in good with my father's team.

Maybe I've been looking at all this the wrong way. Instead of getting insulted that men are using me to get to Father, I should be grateful that they're planning ahead. It's all about attitude and maybe that's why I couldn't find a guy. My attitude sucks.

"Why so glum? Aren't you excited for this date?" Khane asks.

For a second, I stare into his amazing blue-green eyes. His pupils glow slightly with a faint purplish hue. So exotic. I've never been more aware of the light green flecks in his eyes. And no, no I'm not excited for this date. I'm actually more excited to have my pretend-date with Khane afterward.

In the beginning, before we'd all become friends, Tonnie had mentioned that Khane was on the space station to mend a broken heart after catching his fiancée with another. I'd vowed to do anything I could to help him. I still can't believe that someone would have cheated on him. He's amazing—worldly and intelligent. So handsome and elegant, and while his bodyguard is massively muscled and large, Khane is just as much so. Except he's even more handsome than Tonnie with his black and silver hair. And secretly, I prefer the red and white stripes.

"Well, maybe not. I mean, it's kind of embarrassing that my father had to find him for me."

"Hmm. But it's not your father dating him," Khane says softly, reaching for a lock of my hair and winding it around his finger. I love that. I love that we're so familiar with each other. "It's all you, *inca*."

"But what if I ruin it? And like the others, it doesn't go past the first date?"

"If you like, I can prepare you. You can practice your wiles on me."

There's a sudden slam of heat that hits deep in my core. I stare at him, unable to say a word. Does he know what he's saying? Khane smiles and taps my chin, closing my open-mouthed gawk.

"Is the idea really that abhorrent, then?" There's a sharpness behind his words.

Oh, no. I just struck him where his cheating ex did. In his greatest vulnerability, someone not wanting him. And that's not it at all. What had really shocked me is how much I want it.

"No, it's not that. I'm more comfortable with you than anyone. I just didn't want to remind you of your heartbreak."

"Tonnie's been talking?"

"Just that much. You had a fiancée."

Khane nods. "It's true. We came here to get away from the gossip of me finding my fiancée tussling between the sheets with her own bodyguard. But one day I'll have to go back."

"You will?" For a moment I wonder if everyone on their planet has a bodyguard, but then I'm distracted by the idea that he'll leave. That had never occurred to me. I thought Khane and Tonnie would be around me forever, I guess. That where they moved, I'd follow. Or where I moved, they might. That was probably foolish thinking.

"Yes. But that's a thought for another day. Let's get you practiced for tomorrow, eh?"

"What do you mean?"

"I want you to see the way a male should gaze at you. Like this."

Instantly, his eyes turn heated. An unexpected gasp falls from my parted lips. An attentive Khane is lovely and part of me believes that he means it; the focused, dedicated gaze fixated on me. That I'm the one who's caught his interest.

"If a male doesn't look at you like this, he's not worth it. Understand?"

Bemusedly, under his spell, I nod.

"He should make you feel like you're the only female in his world."

"The only female in his world," I repeat. His lips are so full. What would they be like to kiss? Would he kiss me back? Does he ever think of me like that? Would his hands caress my back? Cup my neck?

I'll bet he would be an amazing lover. Intent on pleasing a woman. Completely unlike most of the men on the app.

But that's unfair. That's generalizing.

"He wants a goddess. And you are his goddess. He'll offer you immeasurable wealth, shower you with love and affection, and be prepared to know that your needs must always come before his."

"He sounds perfect," I breathe, and by *he* I mean him.

"Not he. You. You are perfect, *inca*."

I shouldn't be feeling deliciously squirmy inside.

"You see, you're going about this all wrong. You're trying to find a male you can love. No. You need to find the male who will love you." He skims his index finger down the middle of my forehead, the bridge of my nose, and lightly taps the tip. "Craves your smile and your kiss. Loves the way you talk, you laugh. Your cute, old-world expressions that mean nothing to the average masses but makes him—your person—chuckle."

Khane always chuckles.

"A male who wants to please you. A male who fits every single quality you listed on your app." His head turns slightly to the left. "Which is what?"

Still slightly dazed with his attention, I look down at my com and bring up my profile. When it comes up, I begin to read. "*Single Earthian female seeking companionship and an open-minded individual. Only compatible species may apply. Wealth is appreciated and may move you higher up the list, though not necessary. Looks are necessary, or at least serious muscle tone. Sincere applicants only.*"

His lip twitches. "Single Marjian male with a nest egg right here. Looks aren't to be sneezed at—"

I snicker when he uses one of my phrases. I'm rubbing off on him.

"—but in case my looks aren't to your standards, I do have serious muscle tone."

Playfully, I run my palm up his arm, stopping to squeeze at the bicep. "Hmm."

"Well?"

"I'm thinking. Give me a second."

His deep, throaty laugh curls my insides. I'm giddy, staring into his dilated pupils. "There's only one thing left to figure out."

"What's that?" My voice is breathless, following the curves of his lips. Do I dare lean in?

"Compatibility."

A whoosh hits my belly. Is he serious? Or still showing me what I should be looking for? Does he mean we might be compatible? He licks his lips and maybe, just maybe, he isn't showing me what I need to look for in another. Maybe he means him.

"There are my roomies. Ignoring me as usual." Tonnie stumbles and falls halfway into our laps. In the blink of an eye, Khane catches him.

"Oh, my," I say, jumping back. "What's happening?"

"I'm not sure," Amelia says. "He had three watered-down wine spritzers. Maybe someone slipped him something?"

"What's in this wine spritzer?" Khane asks. "Besides wine."

"Club soda. Sometimes a slice of lime."

"I think she likes me," Tonnie says loudly, cupping my cheeks in his palms.

"Oh, boy." I scrunch up my face. "Let's use our indoor voices so she doesn't know we know."

"Carbonation," Khane says. "Carbon dioxide. Our systems can't process it."

"There was no carbon *dockshide* in my drinks!" Tonnie says loudly.

"It's tasteless," I whisper to remind him of his indoor voice.

"Well, good thing we're staying," Khane says.

"Good thing you're staying," I say at the same exact time. We look at each other over Tonnie's head and grin.

"Jinx," he says and holds out his extra-pinky finger. I lock mine to his while Tonnie rolls his eyes.

"No one else understands that," he says. "I did it to Amelia and she looked at me like I was crazy."

"You are," Khane assures him.

"Oh, that's a real thing?" Amelia asks, a frown marring her perfect features.

"It is in Candace's land."

"Candyland," I snicker.

Poor Amelia looks confused.

"Time to get you upstairs," Khane says.

"What?" Tonnie says. "I wasn't done impressing her."

"Oh, I think you impressed her enough," I whisper.

Amelia's face is in her app, frantically making notes. Tomorrow everyone will be warned about the dangers of wine spritzer to Marjians.

Khane drags Tonnie out before he can embarrass himself further and I mutter a quick goodbye to Amelia, who looks like she's a little sad that we're leaving. Maybe she doesn't want to be left on her own—well, actually that can't be. Amelia is fine with attending functions on her own. There's not a shy bone in her body.

Maybe she was enjoying time with Tonnie.

For the first time, I wonder if she's just as lonely as I used to be—before Khane and Tonnie became my best friends.

Tonnie sings loudly in the elevator and by the time we get up to my suite, he's lost his steam and collapses against Khane. I take his other arm and loop it around my neck to help.

We stumble down the hall to my room, which opens swiftly with a swipe of my hand. Khane takes him straight to the bathroom and I pull out the sofa, making it quickly right before they return.

"Drop me off here," Tonnie moans, and collapses his six and a half feet of muscles onto the newly-made bed. Spread-eagled across it, he promptly snores.

"Guess he wasn't planning on sharing the bed with you," I say, then move down to take off his shoes.

"I'll scoot him over," Khane scowls.

"Leave him. He'll have a raging headache in the morning. We'll sleep in my bed," I decide. "It's big enough."

"Are you sure?"

"Of course."

What could possibly go wrong?

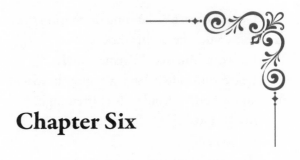

Chapter Six

Khane:

If there had been any light at all in the bedroom, Candace would have seen my *stremma* fully emerged all night long. I turned my back while she slipped into her thin nightgown, and she turned hers while I stripped down. Of course, having nothing to wear, I stripped naked.

Then cursed myself for lying in the sheet completely bare. My cock hardened and my stripes raged like a fever—I became acutely aware of her sweet citrus scent. Her presence so near me that my flesh prickled with awareness. The fact that Candace sleeps like the dead didn't help. In her slumber, she tossed an arm over my chest, then a leg over my waist, narrowly missing the tent of the sheet housing my erection.

What had she said earlier? That she'd heard of my scandal with Fatija. More of an inconvenience because it was made public, an embarrassment to my royal house. Personally, I considered it a relief. I was set free and wasn't the bad person.

Nor was Tonnie. It was public knowledge that Fatija wasn't his favorite person.

The body heat emanating from Candace feels perfect. She's comfortably curled up against me like we've slept together for years. Like this isn't the first time.

How can she sleep? How is she not feeling like me? Aroused? Curious? An unshakeable desire to touch... to stroke her soft skin. Smell her hair, wrap her limbs around me. But she seems to feel perfectly at ease.

Of course. In her dream-state, this is easy. We're friends and comfortable with each other. Candace isn't aware of my feelings for her.

If I could just trick myself into thinking we're an old mated couple and have spent six thousand nights in each other's arms, cuddling each and every night.

Just like this.

I woke right before she did to find the room lightened and her breathing still heavy. She was still strewn across and over my body and I was forced to think of Tonnie in the next room to keep my erection down.

At least my skin was normal colored.

"Khane?"

"*Inca.*"

"Oh my gosh, did I hog the bed all night?"

"Considering you think I'm your mattress right now?" I ask wryly. "Yes."

She gasps... then giggles. "Oh, gosh, I'm sorry. I'm even riding your morning wood."

We both realize what she says at the same time.

She groans and moves to get off me, but I lock her to me with an arm clamped around her waist. My cock is buried between her thighs and I can feel her muscles tense, wrapping me securely within her warmth.

"Don't move," I whisper. "Not yet. Please."

I'm looking down at her sleepy face before she lays her cheek back onto my chest. Her body relaxes while mine throbs with need. The scent of her assails my nostrils—so sweet, so heady, musky with arousal. What is this? A human thing? Surely Candace doesn't want me. Not when she's so busy seeking human males as her mate. When she's consistently set me in the friend zone.

But our hearts are thumping together, beating in tandem as our breathing deepens, becoming more aware of something growing between us. I'm aware of her nipples tightening, poking into my chest. Of her thighs tightening as if she's pulsing her cunt.

Her wet, willing cunt.

Then the thought of her soft skin against mine is too much. With a throbbing groan that I swallow down, I come, releasing what feels like gushing jets of wetness onto our pressed abdomens.

I'm immediately ashamed of myself. I'm royalty. As a prince trained in pleasing females, I should have more control. But I've never felt a need as great as I do with Candace.

Without another word, I gently roll her from me, gather my clothes off the chair, and head into the shower.

Ashamed of myself for leaving her sopping wet with my seed in her own bed.

Tonnie's awake after I dress, so I head into the small kitchenette to make him some coffee. I hear the bathroom door close, and the sound of the water when it starts up. For a second, I wonder if she'll touch herself. Will she relieve the need that she felt?

"Those wine spritzers pack a punch," Tonnie says wearily, not even mentioning that I ended up in Candace's bed.

"Amelia added that little tidbit to the app last night," I say.

"What?" he groans.

"You were quite friendly with her. I think she tried to get you to enter the program."

"Did I?"

I shrug. "Probably. You and she were holed up together for quite a while."

He scowls. "Tricky female."

I open the fridge and study the contents. Apparently, Candace doesn't like to go out to eat and ordered items in because there's a dozen eggs, some cheese, a couple of chopped vegetables from Earth and something else. I pop a pink square into my mouth. It's salty and briny tasting.

"Ham," she says, her hair wet as she appears way too soon in the kitchen. Didn't touch herself, then. "We add it to omelets."

"Is that what these chopped vegetables are for?"

She nods. "We just stir them into the eggs and season." She enters the kitchen, rubbing Tonnie on the shoulder in greeting, and then stands next to me, watching as I crack the odd little white eggs to a bowl. Such a waste of time. Six of their tiny eggs equals one of ours.

She adds salt and pepper to the bowl with the vegetables, working alongside me.

Everything seems back to normal with us and I'm so grateful, I give her a quick smile as I hand her the bowl of pink meat. "I probably shouldn't have popped it into my mouth raw."

She smiles. "It's cured. You're fine."

Tonnie turns green. "Your meat is supposed to be pink?"

"It's okay. You'll love it. Here, I have the perfect hangover cure for you. It's called a screwdriver. Not a remedy to be used all the time, but once won't hurt you. Trust me."

She hands me her whisk and I take over beating the eggs while she gets orange juice from the fridge. "You were pretty cozy with Amelia last night."

"So I heard," he grumbles.

"She's not bad. If you really want her to remove your profile from the app, I'm sure she will."

"I'm sure she'll give me grief and try to change my mind first."

"Well, of course. She's not my father's assistant for nothing." Candace smiles. "But she's not quite the dragon he is, either. Just approach her honestly."

"And tell her I can't hold my liquor?" Tonnie asks, indignant.

"You can't," I remind him. "Now we know to stay away from spritzers."

Candace smiles. "Who would have thought such a mild drink would affect your metabolism like that?"

"We should probably bring up the app and see what attributes have been added to our species," I say.

Candace pulls it up near Tonnie as I finish the breakfast. I'm spreading the plates out when she says, "What? You two are related?"

Her eyes are wide when she looks up.

I give a short nod of my head. I'd always assumed she knew, but how could she? She's not familiar with our culture. "Our history says there are two royal lines descending from the first ruler. The mating was of a king who married twin sisters. Each bore him a son and he couldn't decide who would rule. Normally the first born should, but his first born didn't show any inclination toward it. Instead, the second did. But the first showed an interest in guarding and when assassins infiltrated the kingdom, the older son protected their entire family. From then on, the more prestigious honor fell to the guard of the family. I know other cultures can't understand it and treat the prince with more honor, but that's not how our people think. Now the majority of our families follow the same protocol as that first royal family—one choosing the higher honor of bodyguard for his siblings. Tonnie is my brother. Nowadays, sometimes it's a sibling, other times it's a cousin."

"So, if you had married..."

"Fatija knew Tonnie would live with us and would eventually take a bride. One of our sons would protect the other and more than likely, mine would be born first and train to protect his. Now, of course, it could end up quite different. Say Tonnie entered his profile into the app and is compatible with Amelia—"

His heated protest cuts me off and I can't help but grin, which makes Candace laugh also. It eases my tension that she's not uncomfortable with what happened between us this morning and has the added benefit of distracting her from finding out the real reason why Fatija pursued me.

"Then he might have the first born and eventually when I mate, his offspring will protect mine just as he did me."

"I thought you were close," Candace says with a frown. "I didn't guess you were actually related. Or that your families were so entwined."

"Is that worrisome for humans, *inca*?" Tonnie asks softly.

I hold my breath at her response.

Her face clears. "No, no! Not at all. I'm just berating myself for not asking before this. I must be so selfish. You both know everything about me and I didn't even know you were brothers."

Relief cuts through me. I didn't realize how much I worried that our customs would seem strange to her. Her wrist pings and she glances down at the app, still open in her com. Her face falls.

"What is it?" I ask softly.

"The new person that my father accepted. He's reached out for tomorrow."

"You don't seem excited," Tonnie says.

She shrugs. "I don't want to screw this one up. I'm running out of time."

"How about if you break the rules and take the date at the restaurant of our building?" I ask. "I can sit at the bar for moral support. If you need to ask me questions on what to do, I'll be right there."

"Excellent idea," Tonnie agrees. "And if it should turn out like that Paul the Prick, you can finish the night with Khane. Get some pointers on what might have gone better, or just relax and end on a better note."

"I'd love that," Candace says. "If you're okay with it, Khane. But I can't let this one escape. Not if father chose him."

I don't feel guilty at all as I made the decision to intervene in the date. It's for her own good.

Chapter Seven

Candace:

Date number three. I should be furious. Father had Amelia hack into my profile and accept the invitation to get to know this one before the dinner in which he told me. Instead, I'm baffled as to why I'm excited for this... but then it dawns on me. Each time I have a crappy date, I end up having a wonderful time afterward with Khane. With the first date, he consoled me and told me how awful Paul was for leaving me high and dry in the restaurant. Even called him a *mierjak*, which I assume is the equivalent of an asshole. For the second date, he came to my rescue, and we enjoyed dessert on Brian's dime.

It's the only time we've ever been without Tonnie, as a matter of fact. Not that I don't enjoy Tonnie's company, too. But when Khane and I are alone the ambiance changes between us.

Obviously, since I rode Khane's morning wood.

I think I might be nursing a little Khane crush just in time for the holidays. And it's not my fault. The man has perfect abs, and strong shoulders. Round, hard, strong muscled arms are my favorite. I shouldn't find horns so sexy.

But I do. And I think he's attracted to me—unless a morning orgasm is a natural reaction for his species. I'm confused because if he is attracted, he hasn't done anything about it. Of course, what do I expect? The poor thing was heartbroken by his fiancée. Devastated was what Tonnie had said. The humiliation of remaining a virgin to keep pure just to find her ass up with her bodyguard plowing into her—made more humiliating with cameras flashing all around them. I'm not sure why there was media attention with Khane; in my horror at his humiliation, I'd forgotten to ask. Needless to say, he acts as though we're friends and nothing more. I'm a needy, needy woman because I'm looking forward to anything I can get from him, even if it's just a smile.

As I enter the bar, I head for an empty table, noticing Khane sitting at the front, chatting with the bartender. He gives me a nod and tips his glass toward me.

I give him a finger wave back and... does anyone have the right to look that sexy? He's wearing a button-up, collared shirt today and that does bad things to my libido. I have this mental image of ripping apart the two halves of the fabric and watching the buttons fly as his chest is uncovered and bare... and I lean in to lick.

All at once I'm hot and bothered and as I sit, a server comes out and brings me an ice-cold drink—carbonated water with a hint of citrus, a cute umbrella with a couple of speared not-cherry fruits, and the slight pucker of a lemony alcohol.

"From the hottie at the bar," she says.

"Thanks," I murmur, feeling nervous all at once. Khane's going to be watching me this time.

I hope this will be *the one*—the smoothest date so far. Maybe he'll be normal, not in it for anything except to get to know me. Maybe I won't be awkward and say anything stupid like whether he'd be okay with me remaining friends with Tonnie and Khane.

I nervously gulp my drink, feeling the liquid blaze a fiery trail down to the pit of my stomach. Then I take a couple of deep breaths and think of what Khane would do.

Nothing, and I mean, nothing, would faze him. He wouldn't be nervous over some blind date. In fact, I can't even imagine his father telling him he needs to have a date with someone. Surely Khane gets his own females.

And now there's something a little different in my belly. Not nervousness any longer, that's for sure. No, ugly jealousy rears its head. I wonder what Fatija had looked like? I hadn't cared before but lately, well, how would I measure up to Khane's ex?

I busy myself with choosing my appetizers and drink from the menu bot, noticing that he'd already chosen his own also. I go ahead and transmit the order.

"Candy?"

"Candace," I correct, looking up as the man holds his hand out for me to shake. My father is the only man allowed to call me that and he hasn't since I was in pigtails.

"Apologies." He smiles smoothly. "I'm Dion."

He slides into the seat next to me, all sinewy grace and sparkly white teeth. His skin is lovely, polished and exfoliated, not a hair out of place.

Not hard on the eyes at all.

And yet he looks lacking, and rather round, without horns. Which isn't really fair for this poor man.

"Did you see the latest feature on the app? A compatibility *rating*," he says, his face animated.

I fight an inward groan. Not an Appie. Please not an Appie.

"Together, we're rated nine out of ten stars," he says. "We think alike in nearly every category."

Oh, man. He's an Appie.

I can guess which category is missing between us because I figure a date should be about getting to know each other, not discussing the mechanics of an app which quite frankly bores me to death. I'm missing the technical side to my personality.

"Your father's amazing with this creation," he says. "To think of the heights to which he can take it! With the right marketing and careful financial planning, it can soar—"

"To be fair, my dad didn't do it solely on his own," I say. "He has an amazing assistant, Amelia."

"Yes, yes," Dion interrupts, waving his hand.

I grit my teeth at a complete stranger hushing me. Khane never does that. When I speak, he listens with rapt attention like my words are gold.

A hovering roboserver brings our plates out and we settle them between us. Dion's gaze flits over my choices.

"I'm sure she did a lot of tasks that freed him up for more of his attention on the app. That's what a good assistant is for, after all. But the app itself—the details!" He brings four of his fingers and a thumb to his lips in a chef's kiss. "Perfection! That can only come from the amazing brain of your father."

"So where do you come from?" I ask quickly, hoping to change the subject.

He leans in, checks his com, and presses a button. "Time to get to know each other already? You're on the ball."

Oh, good Lord. He is checking in with the app, a beta feature being tested out with a few of the more quality applicants. The timer—which you click in increments—is supposed to keep you on track to optimize your dating experience.

It doesn't take an Appie to know he's been on the app for a while to be considered one of the more quality applicants to be able to test new features. Maybe it's not a good thing to know he's a regular. Surely if he was a catch, he'd have been snapped up by now?

"I'm the third son of Thomas and Renee Bailey. I have seven other siblings, which is how I'll raise my own sons. Family oriented. They'll be big strapping boys, though I'd prefer ten. That gives way for a couple of girls to sneak in." He wrinkles up his nose. "I'd like them to be close in age, at least ten months apart, though I do realize in reality it'll probably be closer to a year. We'll have to focus on your health"—he pulls away my basket of fries and pushes my side salad closer to me— "to minimize any chances of miscarriage. That would be a complete waste of time."

Gads. Is Khane picking up on all this? I can't let him know that my app personality checked me and marked me for another loser. What will he think about me?

I lean in and smile, aware that Khane's looking our way. I can't help but feel it's more of a grimace, which makes me determined to ignore him from now on. The last thing I need is for him to come over and see for himself how things are going. If he thinks we're doing great, he'll give up and wander upstairs and I'll be left to another humiliating date alone.

"You're no longer a spring chicken so we'd have to hurry. You're built strong, though. Good wide hips. Amply built for feeding our young," he says, looking pointedly at... my boobs.

Khane's a boob man, also. But at least he realizes they're a part of me, not just mobile baby bottles.

Is this how I made Paul feel? Like a crazed stalker planning out our lives? I think back to wondering if he'd be willing to live in my apartment until the kids come and cringe. No wonder he fled.

"You want ten children?" I ask weakly. "That'll keep me pregnant for... like the rest of my life."

"Ten *sons*," he corrects. "And yes, women truly make sacrifices to be good mothers, don't they? I know it'll be uncomfortable at times, but with plenty of exercise and positive thinking, you won't even notice the pregnancy fly by. My mom will have lots of tips. She popped them out like a pro."

"I see." Sensing Khane's gaze, I force another smile. He tries to catch my eye but I focus my attention on Dion like he's the greatest thing since sliced bread.

"And imagine being able to stay home every day to raise our brood. You won't have to work," he assures me.

"Well, that's nice," I say weakly. "But what if I want to?"

He bursts out laughing like I just made the wittiest comment. "Trust me, darlin'. You won't have time. You'll be planning our meals, homeschooling the little ones, hell, laundry alone will be constant."

"Well, it's a little too early to start planning our future, isn't it?"

"I disagree. Aren't we getting to know each other? What better spot than this to tell each other the dreams of the future?"

Dreams or demands?

"Besides which," he winks. "I already have your father's approval. I chatted with him a couple of times. I was ecstatic when he reached out to me on his own."

I feel thrown to the wolves. My father didn't mention that he initiated contact.

"Candace? Is that you?" From near the table, Khane holds two wine spritzers, and sways slightly. He sets the full one down near me, and his half-empty glass nearly sloshes over as he takes a drink, still peering at me over the rim. But then he sets it down, parking it at a spot near me, and folds his strong arms over his chest, glaring at me with a dour expression. There's the faintest, barely-existent shadow of his *stremma* emerging. But why? I know this isn't jealousy. He's never met Dion before.

"Khane. Uh, hi. This is Dion. Dion, meet my neighbor."

Khane pulls up a chair from another table and joins us. Seeing him up close with his powerful body, his majestic horns, and his sharp cheekbones make me flush with heat all over.

"We're on a date," Dion complains.

Oh, oh. Not a good thing.

Ever so slowly, Khane turns to Dion. "I see that," Khane says. Then he flags the roboserver and when it hovers to our table, he presses his thumb to the flatscreen. "So, I'll pay."

From his angle, whatever Dion sees on Khane's account on the screen makes his eyes widen and his protests stop.

I'm curious, but still a little bemused. Surely Khane saw the state Tonnie had gotten into from wine spritzers. Why would he choose them? And how many had he drunk at the bar.

"For you, *inca*," he says jovially, nudging the second glass toward me.

"Thank you," I say, lifting the spritzer and taking a sip. At least it keeps him from having another.

"So, *Djon*," he slurs and slaughters his name. "What do you do for a living?"

With Dion's life plan already laid out, I'm surprised he's willing to allow Khane into our date. But instead, Dion looks as if he wants to impress Khane.

Odd turn of events.

"Dion. I'm a consultant," he says. "A numbers pusher."

He looks like he wants to say more, but Khane's nodding. "Ah, yes, I could tell."

"You could?" I ask, looking at Dion.

Khane continues to nod. "There are subtle clues if you pay attention, *inca*," he says. "This is a professional man who is used to being waited on."

Dion chuckles like that's a compliment. "As I told Candace, my mother would be an excellent model for her to learn from."

I ignore that. "How did you know?" I ask Khane, studying Dion like a clue might pop out at me.

"It's the outer layer of dormant, relaxed muscle. See how it's starting to spread up his thick neck to his jowls?"

Oh. I didn't expect that. I stare at Dion with new eyes. Yes, his neck is a little thick, his cheeks a little puffy. Maybe some fleshy pads under his eyes. Not that I mind a thicker man, mind you. I just don't want to be run ragged taking care of him because he's too exhausted from crunching numbers to mow the lawn. An image of me mowing in the hot sun with kids hanging onto my waist comes to me.

Dion frowns a little but looks over at Khane and decides to suck it up. Maybe he's more broke than I realized, or he's saving all his money for that enormous brood he intends to have and really wants the benefit of Khane paying for our meal. I mean, is that a red flag? Your first date and another male pays for it?

"To be fair, thirty-two is practically middle aged," Dion says. "How old are you?"

Khane leans back rather casually. "Forty-five. I *am* middle-aged."

I can't help but compare the two. Khane doesn't have an ounce of fat on him. There's an intelligence that shines in his eyes, definitely not the sulky frown like Dion wears.

But the *Appie* surprises us. He touches his com and when the hologram image pulls up, he presses a few more commands, then says, "Well, that's why. You have a longer lifespan. Forty-five for you is like twenty-five for us."

"We eat healthier," Khane says. "Exercise regularly. We focus on the mind, body, and spirit." Then Khane winks at me and his words are magically slurred again. "Besides, we don't have male pattern baldness. So that probably gives me an unfair advantage about looking younger."

Dion's nostrils flare and his hand twitches like he fights the urge to touch the top of his head. All at once I notice the top half of his hair is a shade darker there. Maybe it's not actually his.

"Khane," I say, "have a bite of my roll. It might sop up some of that spritzer you drank." I expect him to pick it up off my plate, but to my surprise, Khane leans in and opens his mouth like a bird, expecting me to feed him. There's a devilish glint in his eye and I realize that he knows Dion will never suspect that it's odd for a grown male to be hand-fed. How does he know? Does Khane have excellent hearing? Was he aware of the entire conversation as Dion and I got to know each other? I smile and stuff the entire roll in his mouth, effectively shutting him up.

His eyes narrow. While he chews, I turn my attention back to Dion.

"You're only here for a couple more days?"

He nods. "Unfortunately, they're filled with work events. Although I'd hoped to squeeze in a presentation with your father. Do you think you can help me get in?"

Wait a minute. He's too busy to spend any more time with me but he'd like to squeeze in time for my father?

Khane begins choking on his roll and I pat his back while he reaches for my water glass. Yes, I'd been drinking water with my meal with Dion. He'd frowned at everything I ordered, already thinking of the cleansing my body would need for our future children.

"No, I can't get you in," I say and watch as Dion's lower lip juts out in a pout.

I tilt my head to the right, trying to decide if he's doing it purposely because he thinks it's cute. Or worse, maybe it's a real pout and he does it often when he doesn't get his way.

"Something's wrong with his lip," Khane says, and I turn to see his head is angled in the exact same puzzled position as mine. I start to laugh. Khane and I are like two peas in a pod sometimes.

Dion leans over the table, his eyes narrowed on me.

"Oh, I'm laughing because Khane's head was tilted the same way mine was," I try to explain.

"Maybe it's because you and your neighbor are both drinking the same alcoholic beverages," Dion says, his eyes on my glass.

"If you're this controlling on the first date, I can't imagine what it might be like on the second," Khane says, leaning back, all traces of his slurring gone.

"Khane!" I say as Dion huffs.

Khane frowns and turns to me. "Surely you aren't considering him?"

"My father used the app to calculate our chances of success," I murmur. "I'm sure we might have some rough patches that we'll work through."

Does Dion look a little over-the-top triumphant? As if Khane is a mortal enemy? I'm not sure what makes males posture around each other, but it's not an attractive look.

"I resent having to share my date with him," Dion pouts. "I think it's time your neighbor returned to his home."

Khane opens his mouth.

"Well," I say, before Khane can speak in that imperial tone. "Khane and I watch out for each other. Since he's had a little too much to drink, I'll need to make sure he gets home safely. If you'd rather wait here at the table while I do that?"

He doesn't respond right away, just continues to scowl.

"Or we can sit here and continue our meal and Khane will understand that we need to get to know each other."

Hopefully Khane understands the warning to play nice.

"Exactly why I must strongly suggest that you refrain from alcoholic beverages," Dion sniffs. "There's an old trick, you know. You simply order the mildest form of drink—"

"Like a wine spritzer?" I hold up the glass Khane brought me.

Dion nods. "Yes, and instead of drinking from it, you merely wet your lips with it a couple of times and hold the same glass all night. No one is ever the wiser."

Khane leans back, his jaw tight.

I raise my brows and toss back the contents of the glass in one gulp.

Dion's mouth straightens into a line. "I think you might want to try a little harder to make things work, Candace. Defiance is never pretty. I hope our children don't get that trait from your half of the genes."

"On the contrary, some believe independence is the mark of royalty," Khane murmurs. He flags down the human server, who bounces right over. She's one who serves me, Tonnie, and Khane often and smiles right away.

"Sir Melak'sian, what can I get for you?"

"The usual, please."

"One Marjian *kishiani* coming right up."

Dion holds his tongue, but I can see he's the type of male who can't let it go. Dion scrapes the floor by scooting back his chair.

Then it dawns on me how to get Amelia back for helping father hack into my app. I lean forward. "You know, let me com you my father's assistant's personal number. I'll bet she can get you an appointment with daddy." I wink at him, and his sudden beaming smile makes him look younger.

Khane scowls. Well, well, well. My Trekkie isn't as drunk as he pretends. I kick off my shoe underneath the table and run it along his ankle... the way I'd meant to with Paul before he'd run scared.

Khane gulps and throws back the rest of his spritzer. I cover my mouth with my napkin because I can't control the twitching of my lips.

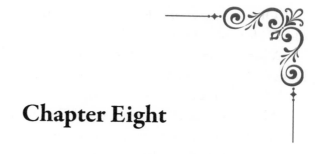

Chapter Eight

Khane:

I shouldn't have tossed back that spritzer. I intended to do as her date suggested and hold the thing to appear less threatening. I thought perhaps Tonnie was weak, but the drink does pack a punch. Or maybe it's Candace herself that packs a punch.

Somehow my chair is scooted up against hers, my thigh absorbing the heat from her leg. And when she touches me with her delicate foot? All the blood in my head disappears and shoots down to my cock.

"Candace will need a date for her father's release party. If you don't live nearby, would you be able to return to escort her?"

"For her father's new app release? Of course. I'm a beta tester," he says, leaning in with his eyes gleaming. I hope that Candace catches that he makes himself available for her father, not for her. "I can put in for vacation time right now, but I think it would make better sense to take a job in this district and have the flight paid for."

He leans back as if proud that he's made such a wise business decision. Two birds with one stone. I wonder how many more of those decisions he'll make throughout their life together.

And with less control over my emotions, or the thought of these two making a life together, the base of my neck heats and I can feel my *stremma* emerge.

Or perhaps it's her soft foot touching my ankle.

"Of course, even if I don't make it on time, I can always meet her there." He winks at Candace. "Since I'll be there anyway."

What does she need him for? A date in which she drives herself and looks for him there? Pretty sure my *stremma* glows brightly right now.

"Ma'am?" The server asks. "What can I get for you?"

"I'll have the same," Candace says. "The *kishiani,* please."

"Thank you," the server says, tentatively. "And you, sir?"

Dion leans back. "What do you have for humans?"

Candace huffs, and in a telling sign, covers her mouth with her napkin. "The *kishiani* is very good, Dion. It's meat and vegetables in a thick sauce, delicately spiced. It's their specialty."

"I'll have the spaghetti," Dion says to the server, who nods and leaves. Then he turns to Candace and scrunches his nose. "I'm not adventurous with unfamiliar foods. And I have a sensitive stomach. My mother can show you quite a few recipes I'm used to."

A booming laugh escapes me.

Then I realize he's serious. He scowls and Candace's lip twitches. So, I straighten my features. "In my culture, when a couple gets to know each other, they don't speak about how their future will be run on the first date. Instead, they focus on growing their attraction into love. Again, as a couple." I turn toward Candace. "I would tell her how beautiful she is. How soft her hair is. How the violet of her eyes matches the shade of an exotic flower." For a moment I'm lost in the depths of her gaze, the dark fringe of lashes a perfect backdrop to showcase the color.

Dion leans back. "Well, I guess it's a good thing our culture is human, right? Because it makes more sense to us that we focus on planning the future and let the love grow later."

"Is it?" But I'm not asking him. I'm still facing Candace.

"A girl likes to be told she's beautiful," she says softly. "She likes to be wined and dined. She wants the giddy, exciting feeling of falling in love with an amazing male."

"Man," Dion corrects.

Neither of us look away from each other. Not until the server bot rolls up. Each dish is marked by the place setting at the table, but we don't need that. We already know that the two dishes that are the same belong to me and Candace, and the strange food of bloody worms piled into a heap with a side of testicles belongs to him.

Along with a side of garlic bread, which Candace and I both reach for, laughing. We usually order a side of the human food to dip into our *kishiani,* which Tonnie finds disgusting.

But he's not opposed to breadsticks.

"We should order one to go for Tonnie," Candace says, on the same track as me. "But we'll eat all the bread."

"He'd appreciate it."

"Do you visit their apartment every night?" Dion asks.

"Oh, yes. We share a balcony. The wall between us needed replaced, and when they removed the old one, we were all so entranced with how much bigger it looked that we demanded they leave it be," I say.

"Ahh, but then you came up with the idea to talk them into using the money they saved to add backlights and shade trees." Candace is positively glowing.

"Well, you are lovely after all, aren't you?" Dion says softly.

As if he just noticed. It's then that I realize my mistake. Instead of showing Candace what he's lacking, I'm showing him how to treat her.

But again, I give him too much credit. Because I'm going to wine and dine his date from right under his nose.

"Another drink, *inca?*" I murmur.

"Only if you're having one," she says.

I hold up two fingers toward the bar and the human server rushes two drinks out.

"Would you like me to leave the roboserver unit here, sir?" she asks me, proving that I've completely taken over as the lead of their date. "You can request anything you need through it, and I'll bring it right over."

I smile and it's one I've perfected over the years. The one that makes mothers push their eligible daughters toward the future king. "That would work fine."

"I'm going to need more garlic bread," Dion scowls, looking at the plate that Candace and I confiscated.

"Please send a serving of bread out with the roboserver," I say to the server, giving her a casual wink as if we're pacifying a toddler.

She titters and I turn back to Candace in time to see her eyes narrowed.

She's jealous. Because I winked at our server? Hope swells in my chest and makes my *stremma* neutralize. She does want me. I had misgivings back at the bar when she would deliberately turn away and not meet my eye. It was like she was dismissing me. But after meeting this *mierjak,* I know there's no way she's really interested in him.

"Yes!" Dion exclaims, looking down at his com. "Your father's assistant squeezed me in for tomorrow morning. Perfect timing!"

The server bot floats around and parks itself at our table.

"Ahh, that's right." Candace smiles tightly. "I think he has a trip scheduled for Ophelia in the Porthouse Galaxy."

"Ophelia of the Triplet planets?" Dion looks up abruptly. "Sometimes those flights leave earlier. He'll have to be at the spaceport an hour before takeoff."

"No one would mind if you have to exit early," I say quickly. "Remember, I'm footing the bill."

The fool thanks me. Not his date. He tosses his napkin on his plate, thanks me twice for getting the bill, tells Candace it was great to meet her, and leaves the restaurant.

That abruptly.

"Well," she says. "That went about as expected."

"He's interested in your father."

She nods. "And a woman like his mother."

"And are you like her, *inca*?" I ask. I find myself holding my breath as I wait for her answer. If so, she may think she could make this work with him.

To my surprise, she starts giggling. "I'll never be the saint that his mother is. Let's get that straight right now."

I pull up the menu on the server bot. "I think we'll need more drinks."

We end up with a dessert to share also, because why not? It's tradition with Candace and me.

***Candace*:**

We're laughing the entire time I try to explain how the date was going. We switch to wine because the spritzer will floor him but won't do a thing for me.

My com keeps pinging, and when I glance down at it, a bubble of laughter escapes me. "First one was Amelia. Second was my dad. Do you suppose they're a little snippy that Dion got an appointment?"

"With that male? I would be."

"Serves him right. He set me up with that nitwit."

Khane looks at me blankly. "Nitwit?"

"Knucklehead."

He shakes his head. "Speak plain Universal, *inca*."

But he's teasing me because I've heard him mutter the words before. Come to think of it, always regarding my dates. It's more like he's encouraging me to use more of my secret phrases. It's a love language between me and Khane. "It's part of my charm, pumpkin."

His brows shoot up in an unspoken question.

"That's an Earth vegetable."

"You didn't actually live on Earth, right? Ever?"

"Well, no. But I watch a lot of vids, Trekkie."

He frowns, but it's a mock-frown, which makes me laugh even more. Because it's my favorite thing to do, I scoop up a bit of the cream with the cake and hold it up for him to taste.

It's a little over-the-top that we share the same spoon. Neither of us say anything about it, but I know we get the same little thrill. It's a dangerous game we're playing.

"Do you want kids, Khane?" I ask, sobering a little.

"Yes." He never hesitates. "You could say I've been bred for them, even to the point of being schooled on how to please a female."

"Excuse me?" I splutter, then burst out laughing.

He grins. "My people believe the bigger the feminine orgasm, the more desirable traits the offspring has. How about you? Want kids?"

I'm still giggling. "Yes, I do too. But it sounds like a woman started that one. A lot of men this age don't care about pleasing, you know."

"Well, I'm older, remember?"

"Are you really?" Because he looks really good.

"No. I was bullshittin' him the whole time."

I laugh at the word he's picked up. When I first met Khane, he was so rigid and formal, and it seemed like only Tonnie could pull him out of that.

Now it's me too.

"What do you mean, bred for kids?"

He traces the elegant pattern of the tablecloth. "On my planet, I'm the Imperial High Prince Melak'sian. There are other princes also, but most people hear Imperial and High and assume I'm the highest."

"A prince?" I ask. "You're royalty, Khane?" Suddenly it all makes sense. Why the crowd at the party oohed and aahed over them. Why the staff at restaurants bend over backward. Hell, even Dion allowed Khane to crash his date.

Oh. My father's excitement at the party.

Khane nods. A tic moves in his jaw. "I meant to tell you. But I wanted you to love me for me. Not for the title."

Love? I get it. That's why his fiancée chased him, although he means love in the sense of best friends, of course.

"Are you the highest, Khane?" I ask.

His *stremma* emerges faintly, barely glowing on his skin. "I was trained to be ruler, yes." But his gaze turns earnest. "It's not a big deal, *inca*. It's just a job, like anything else. One that I receive a lifetime of schooling for. Some would consider that education boring."

He's trying really hard to get me to understand that he's just an everyday person. Why he didn't tell me for so long. Hell, I get deep, dark secrets. I never told him why I'm so hell bent on finding a relationship through IDA.

I cover his hand with mine. "I wish I'd have been there to help you study that boring education. It could have been a relief in your schooling."

He chuckles. "A distraction for sure."

His grin comes easily now and I'm swept away by the beauty of this male. The sharp edge of his cheekbones. The subtle dimple in his cheek that accents the masculine cut of his jawline. Warmth curls low in my belly and I can't help but squeeze my thighs together.

My voice comes out husky and low. "Tell me more about the female orgasm turning out well-behaved kids? Was it a rumor started by women?"

He shakes his head, a huge smile on his face. "Other cultures believe the same thing. That the most perfect kids are made at the time of conception. That pleasing the female should be the primary goal. You

see, the female orgasm is what floods the egg with the hormones required for strength and intelligence."

"I'm targeting the wrong damn species."

His lips turn up in the sexiest smirk. "Tonnie mentioned to turn
your app to target our people, correct?"

"Well, yes, but I've been waiting for Amelia to get all the data entered correctly." And I'm waiting for Khane to decide he's over the train
wreck who cheated on him and agree to enter.

"If you wait, the one male who enters will get snatched up by the
thousands of other females who are waiting."

I snicker. "The one male is Tonnie, Khane. Tonnie."

"Some females think he's attractive. Not that he's ever looked. Part
of that is my fault. He knows I must mate first. And I've been picky,
insisting on Fatija because I knew Tonnie had to grit his teeth when I
ignored his protests. I probably owe him a lot."

"Oh, he is," I say softly. "But he loves you. He would never collect."

Khane's eyebrows raise sardonically. "Don't let him fool you. He
would collect if our mother owed him."

"It might be easier if I was matched to Tonnie," I say wistfully. "At
least he's willing to pretend."

"Is that what you want, *inca*? A pretense?"

Something in his eyes seems intense.

"For now? Yes. You see, I can't get out of making this announcement. I did something foolish, Khane."

His hand covers mine. I take a page from his book, and now it's my
turn to trace the patterned tablecloth as I admit to my failure.

"You can tell me anything. I just told you something big," he says
gently.

"The fancy penthouse apartment?" I blurt out. "I can't afford it.
It was a gift from one of our sponsors—if I would agree to finding a
match and allowing them to use our relationship to be aired as a perfect

match, giving them publicity. I don't have a choice but to choose some-one at the party and frankly, the only one remotely open to it is Dion."

"He's an idiot. There has to be something else we can do."

"There's not. I can't afford to outright buy my apartment at the price they'll suggest—which is throwing the last few years of free rent and interest into the mix."

"You look like you need a hug."

"I do."

"Come here."

I scoot my chair to his. Being wrapped in his arms makes every-thing bad go away. All I'm aware of is his heartbeat and how mine seems to beat in tandem. It takes one split second to decide to press my heart against his.

And they thud together.

We cling together, my breasts mashed against his muscled chest and I can literally feel my nipples harden. My blood is racing through my veins, adrenaline tingling my limbs. Oh, God. I'm turned on, I'm so turned on by this man.

A man who just wants to forget his ex.

Over his shoulder, I look around the restaurant. "I think we're the last ones here."

"We have the cheesecake left. Shall we take it home?"

"Yes. Let's go upstairs and eat it."

"Your place or mine?" Is there a different inflection in his voice? His arm's still holding me tight against him.

I'm going to pretend there is. I'm going to pretend that the double entendre is real and that he's asking for sex.

"Mine," I whisper. "There's no Tonnie at my place."

He gives a dark chuckle that's full of promise and a spike of heat hits me low inside. I think we might be on the same page.

Is it too forward to suggest a one and done?

Chapter Nine

Candace:

The elevator to the penthouse is charged with tension. We're holding hands. Hand-holding, in a darkened elevator because Khane turned the dimmer switch on. Now it's a subtle, sexy ambience that glows all around us.

My fingers throb with heat where his hand clasps mine. I'm desperate to cling to him, but not seem needy. Even if we regret this tomorrow, we have today. This may be my only chance to have him.

There are no words, like each of us is unsure of what to say. Like we're just letting our desires rule, not our heads.

We're both a little drunk on life, on laughter, and on wine when we enter my darkened apartment. I close the door, toss the box of cheesecake onto the counter, and suddenly he stalks toward me, his shoulders so broad, horns majestic.

He's close, way close, and I'm not stepping away.

"I probably should just get going," he rumbles, and his voice is deeper than usual. It doesn't sound like he wants to leave. It sounds like he's letting me choose.

I do something I never have before.

I wrap my arms around his neck.

He lets go of all pretense, and his mouth claims mine. His lips are warm, and he still tastes like the wine we shared earlier, flirting by sharing the same glass, each of us angling it to sip from the same spot.

His fingers are callused when he skims the line of my jaw. His tongue sweeps past my lips, devouring my mouth like he's craved this forever. My heart hammers in my chest as he kisses me, and I want this moment to last.

We're just as greedy as we kiss, hands roving everywhere. And when he cups my ass and yanks me toward him until I feel the rigid length pressing against me is when I realize this is it. This is for real and we're going to do this.

With his other hand, his strong fingers cup my jaw, tipping my mouth up to receive him before trailing kisses down along the side of my neck.

Drugged with the passion that flares between us, I angle my head, so he has better access. He takes his time, tasting my skin and groaning with pleasure.

I'm shivering with need when he lifts his head and looks down at me. "Will this change how you feel about me?"

"Yes... and no. It doesn't change that we'll be friends forever."

"Best friends."

I smile at his correction. "The very best."

"What more do you want from this?" His silky voice is almost a purr.

"One night to scratch the itch and help you get over Fatija."

He pauses and for a second, I think I gave him the wrong answer. Or maybe Fatija wasn't on his mind at all. Maybe I made him remember her. And suddenly I want to take it back, but it's too late.

"But do you want this?" he asks. "Or are you still holding out for a human on your dating app?"

"I do. This thing between us—it's just a little flame that needs to be extinguished, right? A one and done night? Tomorrow the desire will be gone and we'll be able to get on with life as usual? Back to the way we always are?"

He's silent for a while and I think maybe I might have misread things. But then he winds a strand of my hair around his finger and tugs gently. "If you wish, *inca*." And then he leans forward and gives me the gentlest of kisses before picking me up and taking me into my bedroom. "I'll make this good for you," he promises as he lays me out on the bed.

I have no doubts.

I'm propped up on the pillows and can look down as he slowly unbuttons my dress like he's unwrapping a present. I can feel the warm brush of his fingers every now and then, see the gleam in his eyes as inch by inch, my skin is exposed.

"So creamy," he says, placing a kiss right between my breasts. I swear the area tingles from the light, reverent touch of his lips.

When the dress is completely open, all I have left on is my panties and sandals. He leans back and slides my shoes off and then his fingers trail up my legs to my hips. He inserts his fingers into the waistband and slowly peels them down.

"So beautiful," he says reverently. And by the look on his face, he means it. His gaze is glued to my sex.

I open my legs so he can see better, and then I slowly move up, shrugging out of the rest of the dress. I can't stop touching him, dragging his shirt upward, lifting it over his head, almost snagging it on his horns.

His skin is hot to the touch, and I trace one of the beautiful stripes of *stremma* over his abs, up over his chest, to where it curls over his shoulder. "I want to lick you," I admit.

"Not going to say no. Just going to say not yet."

The way he says it makes me angle my head questioningly, silently begging him to explain further.

"I've never had a mouth on me. I won't be able to hold out."

"You've never had a mouth on you?" I repeat, completely baffled. "So, you and Fatija—"

"We did not," he agrees. "Traditionally, a male holds himself for marriage."

My jaw drops. Is he saying *he's* a virgin? I thought Fatija was supposed to be and instead had been sleeping with her bodyguard. I didn't realize Khane was too.

"I'm not without skill," he continues, as if he's applying for the position of my bedpartner. "Part of our training is the pleasing of a female. It's very detailed. We just haven't actually experienced the act itself."

"Training?"

"Six years. I have a *mitrial's* degree." He kisses my shocked lips. "The highest honor."

With the way he kisses, I can believe his training is detailed.

"Wait. Do you want to lose your virginity?" I breathe, as he trails a hot blaze of kisses down the side of my neck.

"Very much. I deserve this, yes?"

"No one deserves it as much as you. But are you sure you want to? With me?" With those words, I look into his eyes, my hands on his belt. The hard ridge of his cock is swollen when my fingers brush against it.

"My best friend? Very sure."

Then we're frantically kissing as I free his cock, stroking it once until I tear my lips from his to look down. I tug the waistband of his pants down and he leans back to help. When he kicks them off his long, muscular legs, he kicks off his boots in the process.

My breath is coming in fast pants. This is so surreal. I'm here with Khane, able to embrace my crush for the first time—the only time—ever.

His legs are all strong, rigid muscles, more of the gorgeous stripes accenting the perfection of his form. His cock is unlike anything I've ever seen; hard, thick with a line of ridged V-shaped muscles on top. There's a hook-like protrusion at the base, on top of his erection, that ought to rub right against my G-spot.

"My fingers will reach it also," he says smugly, taking in my wide-eyed wonder and reading my mind.

"You really are the perfect male," I breathe, and I'm pretty sure the satisfied look he gives is all for me.

"Your pussy is soaking wet," he growls. "Later I'll make you clutch my horns to your cunt as you scream out your orgasm. But for now, can I bury my cock deep inside you?"

"Please," I gasp, wrapping my legs around his waist and kissing his mouth. "Please do. I've been ready for a long time."

So long.

Slowly he pushes into me and gives a ragged groan. I give a shuddering sigh; it feels so wonderful. So deep. So full. I can feel every one of those muscled ridges rubbing against the top of my inner walls, creating pleasurable friction against the sensitive nerve endings. All at once I realize, we're raw. There's no condom, we're skin on skin. But we're not strangers and it's more intimate this way. I arch beneath him, rocking up to meet his thrusts, my hands clutching onto the rounded muscles of his shoulders as his steely heat rubs sensitive areas inside me.

His stripes are so pretty, red and silvery white, growing brighter and brighter with his lust—like a delicious candy cane. I lick up one on his shoulder, and it weaves all the way up his neck.

His shadowed gaze locks on mine. "Nothing has ever felt as good as being buried in your velvety cunt." His voice is heavy with arousal, tight with control. "I'll never get enough of you."

I smile, because we both know the truth. This is one night to get it out of our system, so we can go back to being friends. And to let him get over the wretched female who broke his heart. To show him he matters and she doesn't. To go back to wishful thinking that I might find someone as wonderful as him.

He surges into me harder, deeper. My insides wind so tight I'm ready to explode.

"Yes, like that. Again," I demand. If this feels this good, I want more. I want him to crave this again, and again. Arching closer, I tangle my legs around his waist, locking us together. "Please."

He groans and kisses me roughly. "*Inca*. Tell me you need this."

I do better than that. I catch his face in my hands. "Khane. I need *you*. It's all you."

He fucks me harder, and then he's kissing me, and each kiss is a promise we both pretend we can keep.

I pretend he's mine, all mine. That I'm not about to get kicked out of this apartment for being a fraud, while he can obviously afford his. I pretend we're married, that he doesn't have a strange reason for not being able to join the IDA, that maybe he had joined and the failproof app brought us together. That we're working on making our baby right now.

When he comes, it's with an Earth-shattering roar, his body trembling over me. The guttural, baritone voice that always sounds like walking sex makes me implode on a climax that overtakes me, stars shooting behind my eyes as my limbs tense with the violent orgasm that goes on and on.

When I finally come to my senses, he's kissing my neck.

"You came," he says, and he sounds disappointed.

I huff a laugh. "Well, you did too."

He raises his head, a grin tugging at his lips. "I mean, I hoped to finish you off with my mouth. We'll have to try again, yes?"

"Oh, God, yes."

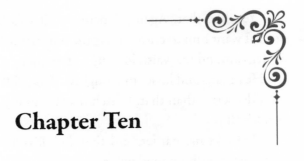

Chapter Ten

Candace:

I'm not exactly avoiding my neighbors. I just need some quiet time to reflect on what the hell happened last night, during which, I guess technically could be called our third date if a gal was so desperate she might count her alone-time with Khane as Khane-dates.

We never slept. After we made love so frantically the first time, we did it again. Slower. And then we showered together, all the alcohol out of our systems, and explored each other with the water dancing along our skin—well, we did it again. Relaxed, more languid, savoring each touch. Each caress.

If I had been in the baby-making mode, I'd have turned out the perfect specimen based on those magnificent orgasms.

When the sun was coming up, he whispered that he had to leave. He had a call from his home planet scheduled. So, we made love once again as a final farewell, both of us knowing our one night was done.

Khane is every bit of what I imagined he would be as a lover. Had I known before this, I'm not sure I wouldn't have jumped in his bed a long time ago. But where do we stand now? I know we both agreed to a one and done but will it be awkward? Knowing what the other looks like naked? Each knowing how the other tasted?

I pull on my swimsuit, grab my towel and sunglasses, and take the back stairs up to the rooftop pool. Not to avoid going by their apartment. Well, yes, to avoid passing by their apartment. When I step out onto the turf, the sun is blinding for a moment. How can it not be? Beyond the temperature-controlled dome of the space station, snow falls. But here, in the fancy penthouse suites, we can enjoy a day at the beach.

"Over here," Khane calls out.

They're here.

He avoids my eyes as he moves to the next chair over, freeing the one between him and Tonnie. Just like old times, the way he used to keep me between them. Is it a deliberate move to keep things the way they were?

I drop my robe to lay out on the lounge chair and while I've done it dozens of times before, now it feels different. Maybe it's because Tonnie is staring straight ahead, lost in his own thoughts. Maybe it's the tic in Khane's cheek as he avoids looking at me, but it feels different, knowing I had my tongue all over him last night. Knowing we shared kisses and caresses and moans and groans.

If I had the chance to experience making love with Khane all over again?

I still would.

"Are you still attending the holiday party?" Tonnie asks.

"Yes. I'm going to announce the winner of my dates. The person that I wish to continue a *long term*"—I use air quotes— "relationship with. Unfortunately, there aren't many to choose from." I suck in a deep breath because this can go so wrong. "And I'll have to pretend that it's wonderful and perfect and cross my fingers that a long-term relationship develops from it because there's going to be so much focus on my life after this launch." I slump against the seat. "I'm counting my chickens before they hatch."

Tonnie snorts at the phrase.

"Your father should never have involved you," Khane says.

"To be fair, I wanted in. They'd asked me." But that was before I met him. In fact, my father had said to consider carefully because if it didn't work out, he wouldn't be able to bail me. Not with a sponsor as huge as them.

"Who'll be next? Now that they've set the precedent for publicizing dating experiences?" Tonnie says. "Amelia?"

"That would be the next good story, right? The app developer's own assistant?" I say softly.

A tic in his jaw works... just like Khane. Tonnie cares for her. I just don't think he realizes it. Maybe Khane doesn't either.

"She'll remain here to get the last-minute details finished for the launch while my dad left for Ophelia this morning."

"Hmmph." But that's all it takes before Tonnie gets up. "Well, I'll see you two later."

Oh, God. He's leaving us alone. Together. And it's awkward. Khane and I go completely quiet long after he's gone, laying utterly still.

Utterly aware of each other.

"Think he's going to see her?" I whisper finally.

"Definitely."

"It's gonna suck to have Amelia claim a match from IDA before me," I say. "Especially since she's not even looking."

"Maybe that's the secret, *inca*. Instead of looking, allow love to come to you."

Speaking of cooking, there's a small brochure in the center of the beverage table next to our chairs that says cupcakes will be served at the upcoming holiday party for the building residents.

Cupcakes.

In one of my library collections, there's a quirky little spell book. It talks about kitchen witches and love spells. Potions and lotions. A plan hatches. A new plan that raises my excitement and gives me renewed hope.

"No time for that. Have I mentioned how important it is for father to succeed? No, I need to take matters into my own hands and I have the perfect idea germinating."

"You do?"

"Mmm. *Cupcake*"—I point to the sign in the center of the table—"that word reminded me of the phrase *the way to a man's heart is through his stomach*. Might be an old-fashioned saying but a good one."

He snorts. "You're going to attract a male through your cooking?"

"In a way. This is more guaranteed than that." I wiggle my spirit fingers, but he'll have no idea what that means.

What spells mean. What magic means. And while some don't believe in it, I don't have anything to lose. It could be real, right? It's the holidays, and the first one starts with the enchantment of Halloween spells and ends with the allure of Christmas charm. I don't want to risk not having magic at my fingertips it if it is real. Excitement bubbles through me. Maybe... it would work on Khane.

"Maybe I'll cure you of ailing from your ex at the same time." That might open him up to being mine.

Unconvinced, Khane just gives a small smile. That's like a challenge... but maybe it's one I can win. Because if Khane can get over that broken heart, maybe he'll see me instead of her, he'll join IDA, I can pick him, and we'll have tons of horned little Marjian babies.

"What are you up to?"

"Just a little hocus pocus. You want to help? I'm going to the library first for research. Then I have to go through my storage unit to find a book I had. Some supplies—"

"No." Khane's voice is clear. "No. I have a lot to do."

Oh. A sense of loss fills me. He's definitely feeling uptight over last night. Maybe he's not over his ex. Maybe he was just caught up in the heat of the moment. Maybe he regrets giving me his virginity.

"Okay," I say, trying to seem casual. Trying not to show my broken heart. In a perfect world, he'd get over Fatija as of yesterday, and look at me with new eyes. "Well, I have a ton to do, so see ya?"

He nods.

Khane:

I stare after her retreating figure. Her hair is piled on top of her head, her delicate spine exposed, the sexy image broken only by the thin pieces of string looped together in the middle of her back, exposing the bare expanse of flesh I'd licked last night. Her delectable bottom is heart shaped and curvy, her thighs thick and strong and womanly.

She is a fucking goddess.

Even the back of her calves are shapely, leaning into slender ankles, with delicate feet tipped by brightly colored toes.

My time is up and except for one night of shared bliss, I'm no closer to convincing Candace that she's mine. That she'll want to up-root everything she's worked for in the last three years and come to a completely different planet and a new way of life, bearing my princely babies.

The last meeting with the board of elders cracked down on my re-turn to Marjia. I have less than a month to sell my apartment.

There's no time left. There's no time to convince her that a human isn't the species of male for her. That only a Marjian Fenal will do. There's no time to convince her that she can have a new life on my plan-et. There's no time to sabotage her dates—not that there was much to do, the losers were seriously lacking—but now I'm down to the wire.

I won't even be here for her holiday—Christmas. Not that it mat-ters because she'll be taken by then, anyway. She's picking one of the id-iots, probably Dion. The moron that wants her to marry him immedi-ately as an incubator for a football team.

I want to send for her, request that she'll visit my home. Maybe even convince her to forgo her penthouse and see if she'll stay. If she's not with child by then, at which point she'll never leave.

My *stremma* explodes—scorching hot with rage—onto my skin at the thought of another male touching her. So much so that I can't even think of a solution that seemed easier when I came up with the plan to sabotage her dates. Last night she may have thought I was trying to forget Fatija, but I've long forgotten her. My plan was convincing Candace how good making love was between us.

Convince her to crave my touch.

Get her to visit my home.

Talk her into staying.

It's not over until it's over. She's here on Inap 8 tonight and I'm also here on this space station tonight. I have some new business regarding the penthouses to take care of in the office, but then I'll see what my adorable—and sexy—neighbor is up to.

The only female worthy of taking my virginity. My future queen.

Had she been of Marjian descent, she would have seen that sign.

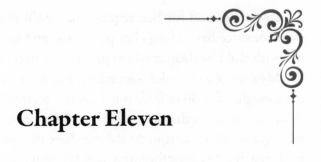

Chapter Eleven

Candace:

"Candace!"

Khane's voice booms from our balcony. He's already halfway through the patio doors—my patio doors.

"Khane," I respond softly, once he's over my threshold. He aims straight for the kitchen.

"Why does it smell like pet food in here?" Khane asks, a frown on his face as he wrinkles his adorable nose.

Gah, I have it bad.

"New plan." I continue stirring the cauldron of... well, herbal tea right now because I'm practicing. I think it smells a little like marinara sauce, actually. Or it would if the sage wasn't so strong. Come to think of it, there's something in the pot that isn't too pleasant smelling. A little like rotten egg. Perhaps I've gotten used to it.

He sighs, which makes me raise my brows at his impatience.

"Well, pardon me if my apartment stinks! A little support here," I grumble. "I told you earlier and you didn't want to help. I'm performing miracles." I glare at him. "By myself."

He sighs again. "To be fair, your smell is wafting across our shared balcony. Is this another new species you're aiming for?" He sounds a little irritated as he peers over my shoulder into the bubbling cast iron cauldron.

Is he jealous? I mean, we both agreed on a one and done, right? Or does he want more like I do?

"It's not a new species I'm aiming for. Well, maybe it is a new species. I'm using a new feature of dad's app."

"What feature is this?"

"I'm combining a little bit of holiday magic with the suggested features. The way to a man's heart is through his stomach. So, baking time with my own twist. I'm baking some—get ready for it—holiday spell muffins. Love muffins, to be exact!"

"And attracting a new, dog-like species? Because it smells like a puppy chow factory."

"No!" I scrunch up my nose, wondering why he doesn't get it. He's normally the smart one of us all... but that was before I slept with the handsome bastard. "The smell is from the spell to add the holiday magic to the recipe. It'll dissipate before someone eats one."

I hope.

"Spell?"

"Yes! See, All Hallow's Eve falls right before Christmas, yes?" At his blank look, I answer for him. "Well, I think so. If I remember my holidays correctly. So, it's a powerful time to create magic... and what better place to direct it than Christmas itself!" I exclaim gleefully.

"I don't understand all your Earth holidays. All Hallow's is a magic one? And Christmas is a loving one?"

"Well, yes. Kinda. Christmas is more like universal love. Valentine's Day would be couples love, but that's not until next year."

He looks exasperated. "Then why wouldn't your father have released his app then?"

"It's all about marketing. He'll need a new theme for that holiday because we're using Christmas as gift giving time, remember?"

He shakes his head. "So, you market your holidays. Each and every one."

"Well, yes." I tap my forehead, sure I'm forgetting something in the grand scheme of things. "I can't remember exactly when All Hallows Eve was. We left Old Earth when I was six. And this galaxy is too far away from planet Earth's internet data to perform a decent search. It would be nice if we had universal libraries, which is basically what dad's dating app is turning into."

I can tell he looks skeptical at the far-fetched idea, but that's because he's not into dating apps. Funny thing is, the dating app managed to make him and I aware of each other. Even now, my girly parts would be purring because Khane's in my kitchen. Except for the godawful smell. I flip on the air purifier and a soft hum whirrs up the stove.

"I do remember three holidays were really close together. Like blam, you'd put away the decorations for one and pull out the decorations for the next. Anyway, close enough. I'm pretty sure it falls on the last day of October, right before the Christmas holiday in December. I don't think I'm missing another holiday... something in November, though to be fair, different areas on Earth celebrate different things at different times. And it's not always Christmas for everyone, which is why we say Happy Holidays. To encompass everyone and all the various holidays."

"Well, I'm sure that's close enough then. You really think this is going to work?"

I nod. "Proof's in the pudding, naysayer. You'll see."

He scowls and it's rather adorable. I have to fight the urge to use my fingertip to rub the line from between his brows. "What is this magic spell?"

"Are you going to help?" I ask, glad everything is good between us again. I'm sure my eyes are shining with love because Khane looks taken aback.

"Yes," he says softly, tucking a loose strand of hair around my ear. "I'll help."

Aww. There it is. We're back to normal. I can't control the huge smile that hits me. My heart feels like it'll burst in my chest. I have it bad for this alien who wants nothing more than to get over his ex. And I should be helping him with that, not focusing on a Khane-sized crush. When I have to pick a boyfriend, a real boyfriend, I'm going to be so disappointed.

"Great." He clears his throat. "Let's get started."

"Okay." I smile brightly and I'm sure it's encouraging. "Here's the spell book I found in the library archives. Had to shell out a pretty penny to get it printed, too." I grumble. "Now, I think the proper way to perform magic is to let it work itself. So, I'll just close my eyes and open the book and the exact spell we need will pop out at us."

"Hmm."

My eyes are already closed so I can't see his expression.

I open them suddenly and startle—he's staring right at me.

"Khane! Your eyes were supposed to be closed too."

"You didn't say so," he counters.

I roll my eyes and look down to see which spell the book has brought me. "Perfect! If it had been a snake, it would have bitten me."

He smiles indulgently. "You really need to stay out of those archives. I'm the only one who understands what you mean when you speak."

I ignore him. "As I was saying, the perfect spell popped off the pages at us. A love potion. I'll use it as the wet ingredients for the love muffins."

"Really?" Like a man, he sounds a little skeptical.

"Oh, yeah, baby," I croon. "Let's see. *Ingredients: a small, galvanized tub. Brut body spray, soap, water, cloth, towel, deodorant, toothpaste and toothbrush.* Okaaay, we almost got all those. But I've never heard of the Brut." I squint and continue reading. "*Spritz body spray lightly into the air to set the mood. (Or try essential oils!) Soak cloth in water, apply soap liberally. Wet body, then rub cloth on toes, pits, and all private spots in between. Dip cloth again in tub, apply more soap liberally, rinse well. Repeat. Dry with warmed bath towel. Apply deodorant. Spritz a little more body spray under arms and on neck. Slather toothbrush with paste, apply to teeth and scrub tongue. Rinse out mouth. Smile at your beloved.*" I scratch my head. Awkward. What kind of a spell is this? "Not sure if we're both supposed to do it?"

He sounds a bit strangled. "Would the spell work if we just used a shower instead?"

"I guess?"

"Let's toss the body spray out too. Since you don't even know what it is."

"Good idea. This must be an old spell book because I don't have any idea where to get it. It probably no longer exists, or it's just manufactured on Old Earth."

"And what does any of this have to do with food?" he asks peering down at the page like I've misread it.

"Well, nothing really. Maybe it opened up to the wrong spell? Aha. You screwed it up by not closing your eyes when I picked it!"

"Again, you did not specify—"

"Oh wait." I continue reading. "Actually, it's a cleansing spell. It's to cleanse the aura before performing the real magic!" I smile triumphantly. "Afterward is when we gather the ingredients for the love muffins."

"Love muffins?"

"Yup! I'll slap them in the freezer and the people who partake of the love muffins will be blinded by love. It'll be my test." Maybe I should make sure Khane has one early, for extra potency. I won't even have to pull the rest out of the freezer once he falls in love with me, joins the app, and I pick him.

He claps his hands suddenly, startling me. "Well, let's get started."

"Okay. Skip the galvanized tub... using a shower instead... okay, soap, water... well, everything we need is in my bathroom."

"Should I run next door and get my toothbrush?"

"I have an extra in the cabinet. Let's do this!"

We head into my bathroom and suddenly it seems much smaller with both of us in there. I start the shower so it'll get warm, and then we kind of stand there awkwardly.

Like we're not both aware of what's under each other's clothing. Or maybe that's why it's more awkward. We agreed to a one and done... but I want another shot. So maybe it's just me who's not acting normally. Now that I study Khane—he's leaning back against the wall, arms casually crossed across his massive chest. Waiting.

"Well, let's brush our teeth first, shall we? Get that out of the way?" I ask brightly.

He spreads his hand out toward the bathroom counter. "Lead the way."

I open the medicine chest and grab the spare toothbrush for him, then get out the paste. I dab a little minty freshness onto our brushes and we both start scrubbing, watching each other in the mirror. I lean over to spit in the sink, and he follows suit. Then we brush some more.

"Long enough?" he asks, through a mouthful of foam.

I lean over and spit before answering, which triggers him to lean over next.

"I guess?"

"Don't forgeth yur thungue," he says, swiping his brush across his own.

I do the same and gag slightly. "Gah!" I lean over the sink to spit and then rinse. "There. All done. Step one of the magic... ooh, Khane, I can feel it tingling."

"Do you?" He looks a bit skeptical as he peers down his little alien nose at me.

"Well, halfway." Or maybe it's tingling because... well, the next step. We're going to get naked in front of each other.

A new tingle shoots down my center and I squeeze my legs together. "All right. Strip," I command. Better that he goes first and I can watch.

He raises his brows. "You're the magic master. I would think you'd want to go first so the magic comes to you first."

"Oh. Good point." I take a deep breath and grab the hem of my shirt and yank it smoothly over my head.

First smooth move I've ever done.

Heat flares in his eyes as he studies my breasts, nipples barely covered by the sheer pink bra.

Oh, yeah. Magic's working.

I reach up behind me and unsnap my bra. It comes loose but still covers my breasts. It's almost a teasing shot, I realize as I cross my arms over my chest to reach for the straps on the opposite shoulders.

His nostrils flare like he can't wait for me to pull them down.

Ever so slowly, I inch the straps down my shoulders, first one side, then the other, my arms still crossed, holding the cups up, blocking his view.

He looks like he's about to reach out and yank it off me.

"You okay, handsome?"

"A bit distracted," he admits, his eyes glued to my chest.

Ha. By two boobies instead of three. Take that, Fatija.

"Need some help?" I reach out with one hand to indicate his belt.

We both freeze... me because I feel the giant erection, him—well, I don't know why.

"Are you shy?" I whisper.

"Should I be?" He rips his shirt over his head. "We've already done this once. Are we going there again? Please say yes."

"If the magic demands it," I say demurely, wanting to appear nonchalant. But then I give up the act and give in to my need. With a quick flick, I unbuckle his pants and pull them down to his ankles, going to my knees in the process and letting my bra drop to free my breasts.

"Well, you're a sight for sore eyes," I whisper to his magnificent red cock, curled like a... candy cane.

He groans at my pun.

"I want this," I breathe, right before I lick the head of his cock. He tastes tangy and sweet and I stretch my mouth to get as much of him inside me as I can.

His ab muscles are trembling, his massive thighs twitching as he groans. I want this so bad, I feel slippery wetness gushing between the lips of my pussy.

I let myself slide down his shaft and then I lick my way back to the base, noticing his stripes glow brighter than ever before on his dick. He's grunting and he's groaning, pushing my bangs back from my head so he can see me fully engulf his cock, and I know he's loving this.

"You're so *tafyaking* beautiful, your lips around me. Loving me."

He doesn't say loving *it,* as in the blowjob. He says loving *me* and that shouldn't make me gush more. But it does. I suck harder and cup his balls. I make humming sounds with my mouth to vibrate his cock. And I love this. I love him in my mouth and something inside me knows I can never, ever replace him with another. I'll have to find a new way out of this mess.

"Lick it with the tip of your tongue. Light flicks or I'll blow."

"You blow and I'll swallow," I promise.

I'm not ready for the fierce growl he emits as he pulls from my mouth and hauls me up against him. I can feel him shuddering as he tries to control himself. The hard ridge of his shaft is pressed up between us—the way it was the morning he came all over my belly.

I shouldn't find that so hot. How could I not find this hot?

With one impatient hand, he pushes the skirt and panties down my hips and then picks me up to step into the shower.

"You're so beautiful," he says as the warm water sluices down us. In a show of utter strength, he lifts me against the wall and sucks a nipple into his mouth. I squirm under his touch, my empty pussy clenching at air as his rhythmic pulls make me gasp.

"Beautiful everywhere," he says, pulling away to lift me higher. There's a windowsill that acts as a ledge in my shower and he sits me on it, my pussy wide open to his view. "Are you dripping for me, *inca*?"

"Yes," I groan, guttural and needy.

"Hold onto my horns." The instruction in his voice brooks no argument.

I grip his horns as his mouth clamps onto my clit, and a thick finger pushes between the lips of my pussy, curling deep inside me. This is so hot and I'm wetter than I've ever been in my life.

"Oh, you like that," he says, his voice vibrating against my clit. "You're clamping around my finger so hard, little love. I wish it was my cock there instead."

"Me too, Khane," I breathe. "I want your cock so bad."

"I'm going to make you come like this," he says. "Open, so I can watch your gorgeous little pussy spasm. Then I'll fill you up with my fat cock and fuck you against the wall."

"Yes," I agree, not able to say more as his mouth lowers back down to adore my clit.

My blood is rushing through my veins. This is so hot and I think it'll always be like this between me and Khane. My greatest wish is that we'd be married. That he'd be my husband and we can have this every single day. I will never, ever take Khane, as my husband, for granted. I will treasure each day like our first.

His mouth is scorching hot, his tongue flicks back and forth against the nub in light, tantalizing movements. I reach for his horns, pulling his head to me, keeping him there and not letting him go.

His mouth clamps onto me, sucking so hard it feels like he's wrenching the orgasm from my body.

I explode on a shriek, my back arching and my legs involuntarily clamping around his face.

Her back slides down the wet shower wall, legs open as I hold her ass in the palm of my hands, settling her right down on my waiting cock. I slide into her eager body with little resistance, her flesh tight and swollen and so slick. The head of my cock presses between her perfect, pouty pussy lips and buries into her in one sweep, balls deep, and I see stars.

She's hot and slick and perfect as I hold her up against the wall. Her hands are on my shoulders, stroking my muscles.

"That's it, baby. Fuck me."

Such naughty words coming out of her mouth shouldn't turn me into a raging beast. Is it because she called me an endearment? All I can think about is how this could be ours. If I can convince her to throw away her life here on this space station, her apartment, her dating app, everything, we can be a mated couple. A prince and princess.

Someday, a king and queen.

The thought of that demands I possess her. I pound into her, pumping her full with slamming strokes that make her moan in my ear. "Harder."

In and out I thrust and when I put my thumb onto her clit and press, she shrieks and grinds her hips into circles onto my cock, her pussy clenching in shuddery waves as she climaxes, the waves of her contractions milking my own orgasm. With a roar, I release inside her so hard, my cum erupts from her pussy and hits the shower floor with a thump.

We both breathe hard as I gently let her legs down, then carefully, tenderly soap her body. I look into her eyes, letting her see all the love I have for her, aware that if I say the words, she won't believe them.

All I can do is show her.

Show her that Fatija was just a long-ago spot in my life. That she's the one, with her crazy sayings and her love for strange languages. That she so desperately craves living on the Earth she was born to, and I can offer her a whole fucking planet.

That I can offer her as many babies as the idiot she might have chosen wanted to, but I would never require her to wait on me hand and foot. I would provide her with my help, with nannies, with uncles and aunts and grandparents. Hell, I'd build a palace for her father to live in across the street from us if she wanted.

Not that life as a royal is easy. But I'd be there in her corner to help her navigate our combined lives.

Forever.

"One more time, sexy?" Candace asks. "Then we'll get serious and go back to the kitchen witchery?"

"Anything you desire," I promise, bending my head to kiss her again. The promise feels like more than a simple agreement.

It feels like I'm offering her my life.

After we make her cupcakes, I'm going to tell her of the plans I made to buy our penthouses so she wouldn't have to worry about any more debt. I'll beg her to marry me, tell her how I'll worship her for the rest of her life, and promise her that I'll spend each day making her fall in love with me.

That's a promise I'll keep.

Chapter Twelve

Candace:

"Okay, ready?"

We're more relaxed and ready to create this love spell now that the urgent need between us is momentarily squashed by shared orgasms. Khane might have been fine with lounging in bed the rest of the day, but I need this.

Desperately.

I need to make him fall in love with me. I'll banish Fatija from his broken heart if it's the last thing I do. I'll make him realize I'm the one for him and that we can make little striped babies with adorable horn nubs.

Khane pulls the cauldron between us as I point to the recipe I'm about to read. "Ready."

"*Two unicorn tears.*"

He looks at me blankly.

"Substitutions, sweetie. Tears are what? Salty water? Add two drops of water and a shake of salt."

He does it and then looks into the pot skeptically. Geez, the man has no imagination.

"Well, it's *unicorn*, so maybe sprinkle in some of that cake glitter too."

He tosses some in.

"*Time*. Well, we don't have a lot of that, so toss in a sprig of thyme instead."

He throws it in.

"*A cup of moonlight.*"

This time, the man doesn't blink. He heads over to the balcony, grabs the empty cup I left sitting on the lounge tray from the night before, brings it inside, and dumps it in.

I beam.

"*A pinch of enchanted confidence*. Hmm. Confidence? Use cinnamon. We have plenty of that."

He brings the bottle up to peer at the ingredients. "How do we know it's enchanted?"

"Well, you gotta mutter a little enchantment over it." How is he not getting this?

"May the force be with you," he says and then flings six fingers out, and waves his hand around.

"Perfect!" I smile encouragingly, then continue reading. "*Stardust.*"

"Got it." Khane picks up the candied cupcake sprinkles. Into the pot they go.

"*A wink and a smile for extra charm.*"

He winks, but his smile looks like a grimace. It's up to me to take up the slack, so I offer a big, beaming one.

Then I start to read. "*Begin your mystical journey on a bewitching night, preferably under a full moon.* Eh. This is daytime, but I still feel like it's bewitching."

"Agree."

"*Dress in magical attire, complete with pointy hat.* Ugh, well, I only have one pointy hat for wintertime. Oh, I know! You hold onto a broom. That'll work. Oh, oh. We were supposed to stir with a sprig of enchanted rosemary. Why wasn't that on the ingredient list?"

"Here, use the thyme again."

I stir everything gently with the well-worn sprig of thyme. "*Infuse the potion with the moon's romantic energy. Use plenty of love.*"

Khane and I stare awkwardly at each other. "Are you loving it?" I snip.

"Yes!" He scowls as if he's loving it ferociously.

I turn back to reading. "*Sprinkle giggles of mischievousness into the mix.*"

Khane leans over the pot and barks out some almost maniacal laughter. I add to it and it really sounds like a loonybin in the apartment.

"*Drop kisses into the cauldron and say, 'Calling Mister Right or Mister Right Now.*'"

Quickly I unravel the foil from the candies and drop three in. "Calling Mister Right."

"Calling Mister Right," Khane repeats.

"Khane! You'd say Miss Right." He rolls his eyes and repeats it correctly.

Gah. I love this man and his willingness to participate in my schemes.

"*Sprinkle in more unicorn tears. Let them fall into the cauldron like precious gems. Imagine the tears of joy you will shed when you find your beloved.*"

Khane sighs. "I'll grab the salt."

"Or should we try to use real tears?" I'm worried over how many substitutions we seem to be using.

"I'm not sobbing over a cauldron."

"Really? This is going to bring your perfect lover."

Though he grumbles, he still tosses a couple drops of water into the pot and sprinkles more salt.

"Oh, all right. Now we want to spice it up, so think of the passion we want to ignite while stirring clockwise and tossing in more enchanted cinnamon."

I start stirring. He grabs the cinnamon bottle.

"Wait, what are you thinking of?"

"Something passionate?"

"But what?"

"How I felt when we were naked together."

Oh, yeah. That's good. I nod encouragingly. "Okay. *Stir your elixir one final time, then take a sip. Visualize yourself radiating love and charm, drawing your crush to you like a giant magnet. Imagine your heart beating strong in your chest, attracting your lover with a booming, magnetic pull.*" We both pause while we manifest. "*Now put on your most irresistible smile and wink at the moon. Your potion is complete. Carry it with you to cast your love spell on anyone who crosses your path.*"

I smile at Khane and make a deliberate wink. He smiles back, rather indulgently and gives a wink right back. My heart swells tenderly at my cohort in crime.

"I think instead of carrying it, we'll add it to the muffins, right?"

"If you say so, *inca*."

I dump the box of mix into the caldron. "Grab a couple eggs, will ya?"

He goes to the fridge and when he brings them back, I crack them in, and stir it all up. I pour the batter into muffin tins. On top, I sprinkle on more sugar. "Sweet for love."

Then I dip the spoon into the leftover batter and taste it, offering him a bite. I feel strangely satisfied when he accepts, like I got some of the magic into him and it'll be that much more powerful when we enjoy a finished love muffin together.

And then he pulls me toward him. "Crazy female, don't you know you are the love in this recipe?"

My silly heart flutters wildly. So powerful! I think it's working and that was from just a taste.

"Spell," I correct, just to make sure we're grateful enough to the spell guardians of the book, or whatever.

He presses teasing kisses to my lips.

"What?" I protest, giggling at his nearness. He makes me woozy, like a schoolgirl with her first crush.

"You've cast a spell on me."

"Then it works like a charm," I crow, taking in the mess on the counter. It looks like a tornado hit my kitchen. Hell, it looks like a tornado hit my bathroom. Was. So. Worth. It.

"I love you, Candace."

Whoa. There's a roaring whoosh of air whistling between my ears. Did I hear what I think I heard? The love muffins didn't even have to bake. They're that powerful.

He lowers his head and I raise mine, eager to be spellbound too. Or, hell, just eager for the taste of his lips.

He's mine. I want his kiss now that we belong to each other. Because he loves me and I love him and I'll tell him as soon as we're done kissing.

"Sorry to interrupt."

We both jerk our heads toward the balcony where a grim-faced Tonnie pauses at my patio doors.

"What's wrong?" Khane asks.

Tonnie crosses the threshold into the apartment. "Official word from the palace. It's time to go home. Now. They've sent a ship."

Khane swears under his breath. "But we're not due—"

"There's been an emergency so they sent for us early."

He's leaving.

They're leaving. I stare at Tonnie in horror.

Wait. The muffins are working even now. If he could just give them time to bake—

But Khane has morphed into someone I hardly know. His spine has straightened, his shoulders thrown back like a majestic ruler. Not like a man who loved me so thoroughly a few hours earlier. Not like a man who winked at the moonlight and made unicorn teardrops.

"Khane?" I whisper, my voice quivery and unsure.

"I'm sorry, *inca*. I have to go."

"But... you and me—"

"I'm sorry. I shouldn't have waited so long. Now it feels like there isn't any time to tell you—"

"—there isn't," Tonnie says, looking down at his com.

Suddenly I remember all the times Khane told me he couldn't join the app. He couldn't be one of my dates—yet his virginal ass slept with me. "Why did you wait? Were you stringing me along?"

Khane's jaw clenches. "To show you every human you date is a loser unworthy of you. To show you that you are a Marjian at heart, if not by birth."

"I'm missing the third boob," I say quietly.

"I like two boobs," Khane says flatly.

"Me too." Tonnie agrees. Distracted, we both turn our heads toward him.

He shrugs.

But Khane's a prince and has to bring home a princess. "Wait a minute. Do you mean my dates were set up?"

"No! You were doing a rather good job of picking the losers. I just helped you to prove that none were worthy of you."

"So, all this time, I had a chance at finding a real match?" I ask, horrified that he wasted my entire lease.

"Yes," he says. "Because none of those losers are good enough for you. I revised your dating profile for you, *inca*. Do you want to know what it says?"

I nod, still shocked and betrayed that he's set me up.

"*Single Earthian female with the beauty of a Goddess seeking an undeserving insignificant male to worship her in the way she deserves to be worshipped. He must be royalty, with a lifelong bodyguard, offer her immeasurable wealth, shower her with love and affection, and be prepared to know that her needs will always come before his.*"

Tonnie sighs. "That's so romantic. Unfortunately, we gotta go."

"Wait for me?" Khane says, ignoring Tonnie. "I will make it back to you before you have to choose. I will fix everything, I swear."

He can't fix it. I'll be responsible for paying the apartment if I don't follow through with choosing, but maybe I don't mind. Maybe I can get a job on his planet and pay off my debt over time. Suddenly the future doesn't look so bleak.

Not with knowing the man I love wants me too.

"Will you?" he asks. "Will you trust me?"

"Khane," I whisper on a ragged sigh. "I want this too."

And even though I should be mad, I should be furious with his thwarting my every date, I should demand respect—the way he taught me—my heart melts at that dimple in his cheek, the way he looks so worried. The fact that he gave me his virginity, a gift he can never give anyone else.

"*Inca*," he groans and it's against my skin, his breath warm and sweet, just before his hard mouth captures mine, kissing me like we've kissed a thousand times before. Like it will never be our last.

And no kiss has ever been like this. It's like my life depends upon this, like my heart will never be owned by anyone else, like it would stop beating if he stopped stroking his tongue against mine. I cling to him, my hands on the rounded muscles of his shoulders, trying to press closer for a deeper taste, my pulse pounding in my throat, and between my legs.

My eager response is answered by a groan and immediate stripes that break out on his skin, a faint glow of white stripes that signal arousal and the red flashes that show lust. His *stremma* is instant and in full force, not like before when I'd only had brief glimpses that grew in strength.

"Khane." The words fall from my lips on a needy moan and I'm not sure if I'm begging or pleading or just want to utter his name.

"I have so much to tell you, and no time to do it. I'm a fucking *mier-jak* because I never wanted any of your dates to work."

"Every date worked. At the end when they left and it was just me and you," I say.

Tonnie clears his throat.

"One week," Khane says. "Give me a week and I'll be back, okay? I'll go to your function with you and you can announce that you're no longer enrolled in the app."

Bemusedly, I nod. "Absence makes the heart grow fonder, you know."

He chuckles and leans down to kiss me one last time. "I love your witty phrases."

"Time's up. The ship's here," Tonnie says, looking down at his com, and just like that... they're gone.

In the blink of an eye, their bodies shimmer and fade out, my arms falling as I clutch empty air where Khane had stood and now has disappeared.

For a second, I wonder if I dreamed the whole thing. I eye the poured cupcakes warily, especially the one where Khane and I each took a test bite. Maybe it caused a massive hallucination? But I'm not sure if it was good or bad—I mean, Khane said he wanted me to choose him. He wanted me to be his. He'd come back. Would make my every dream come true. I don't want to have hallucinated all that.

In a flash, I take off out of my French doors, across the balcony, and push my way into theirs.

It's completely empty, a vast void of any and all presence of everything Marjian Fenal.

It wasn't a dream.

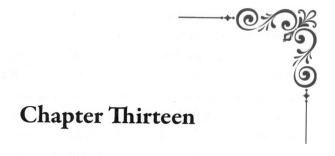

Chapter Thirteen

Candace:

He never came.

The Christmas tunes that play softly in the background sound hauntingly sad and full of misery, instead of imparting the usual Christmas cheer.

That last day in my apartment, when all traces of my friend and lover instantly disappeared, when Khane promised he'd be back in a week, seems like it never existed. He never called, never wrote, never returned.

He stood me up. And while I have no idea how to reach him or where he's gone, he's known all of this time just where I am. Because I haven't stepped foot out of my apartment since he left, desperately afraid I'd miss him if he beamed down from wherever again.

What did I expect? He's a prince, and despite what he might have felt for me, he probably got home and realized it could never work. And once again, I'm faced with the unwanted choice of being forced to pick someone from the app, or face a debt that will take me three entire lifetimes to pay off.

Problem is, I waited for Khane all this time. I didn't look for any new dates, I didn't contact any old dates to see if they'd like to try again... nothing. So, my only option is the semi-interested Dion, the last date I'd had that rushed off to meet with my father. A man who is clearly interested in my dad's company, who wants me to sit at home like an Elf on the Shelf and keep house for him while waiting for him to knock me up every nine months.

Hey, at least with humans I know it'll be every nine months. But what choice do I have? I have no way of paying off the penthouse and I can't tarnish my father's reputation by letting bad press announce I'm bankrupt and in default of my own agreement. How I wish I'd listened to him when he told me it was an expensive venture. But I had stars in my eyes at the thought of living in the lap of luxury. And while that lap of luxury at least introduced me to Khane, now I know I'd live in a hovel if it was with the man I love.

I'll have to choose Dion today.

The lights in the conference room dim enough for the hologram features on the main viewing screen in various colors to show. The hologram podium lights up in flashing colors of red and green to celebrate the Earth holiday. A blinking candy cane with a red velvet bow tied around the center makes me want to weep.

Not even the beauty of the lights cheers me up this season.

My father walks onto the stage. Behind him filter in his sponsors and I want to shrink down in my seat at the sight of all those shark-toothed suits that smell of wealth and greed.

I should have listened when my father said the penthouse was too expensive. Because yes, now it feels like a fancy jail cell.

"Thank you all for coming. Let me introduce our sponsors."

Each man steps forward when his name and business is announced, says a few words, and then walks right past me on their way to fill up the empty seats in the first row next to me. I fight the urge to shrink further down in my seat. Finally, my father stands at the podium again.

"As you know, IDA has had upgrades that make dating easier than ever. A compatibility rating which tells you how alike you and your pre-selection will be based on a series of questions and data each person provides. Next, we've implemented a guide feature for those of you who are unsure of the next step in the dating program with other species."

On the screen behind my father, a slide of the latest feature in the app appears.

"You can set it up in advance, entering the species of the date you'd like to impress. For instance, one tester recently reported—"

In front of us, the camera shows a view of the audience. Right smack in the middle of the sea of faces, Dion raises his arm in a weird, fist-bump kind of motion, wanting to be *the early bird who catches the worm*, and make everyone aware of his presence. Cocky and self-assured, because he knows I sit in the front seat and have to make a choosing from my lack of available sources.

Father smiles. "Dion Brown reported programming his for a series of gentle reminders of what area in the date he should be in. For instance, after the introduction of the date, as they made small talk and dropped their first impression barriers, his app buzzed with an alarm that told him he should be moving on to the next stage. The getting to know each other phase."

I try hard not to wince. Gentle reminder? That had to have been the most obnoxious alarm I've ever had on a date. I wish I would have mentioned to father to remind prospective dates to turn the volume down.

And my stupid, weepy heart remembers Khane on that date. I have no earthly idea where he and Tonnie are, but do they ever think of me? I miss Khane with every beat of my heart. I fell head over heels in love with him and I don't know how I can ever bear to let Dion touch me.

But what choice do I have?

"And now, my precious daughter, Candace Jameson, will speak and let us know the answer we've all been waiting for. Who was her perfect connection on Ida?" Daddy gives me a wink, like he knows something I don't. Oh, God. He thinks I'm about to be the happiest woman on Earth—err, Inap 8. Instead it's the most miserable day of my life.

I startle. How long have I been zoning out? My time is already up? My father normally talks for forty-five minutes or so.

Thunderous applause cuts my father off, making me swallow the excess saliva that's pooled in the back of my throat as I panic. I had no idea how popular the thought of the app creator's own daughter running through the dating motions would be.

It's here. The final moment is here. My feet feel like lead as I walk up to the podium he just left, the swish of my green silk dress with silvery white, pencil-thin stripes swishing around my calves. The dress is belted with a red velvet, buckled belt to represent the holidays, but I really picked it because it reminded me of Khane. The silvery white stripes match his exactly, the green are shaped like his stripes, just a different color. A color that would complement him, if he were here.

I look pretty and put together. But inside, I feel more like a Halloween witch than a picture of Christmas cheer. I don't even have the love potion muffins to pass out. I pulled the whole damn tray from the freezer when Khane didn't show, sobbing as I devoured them in a frenzy along with a gallon of ice cream. But obviously no more magic hit, not the witchcraft kind, not the Christmas kind. Nothing.

The room is silent as everyone waits.

"Good afternoon," I say into the microphone. "Thank you for your interest in my personal experience. I've had so many wonderful dates with IDA it was hard to choose." Not exactly a lie. My mind flits to an image of me and Khane after each date, staring up at the stars, sharing dessert, getting naked in my bathroom. All because the app suggested cooking, which led me to think I'd produce love muffins. Of course, I also thought those love muffins were slightly hallucinogenic, but that's another story.

"Who's been the best out of all your dates?" Dion calls out, making several people around him snicker.

Lord, he's already running my life. He's been talking to those around him, then. Telling them he's the shoo-in to be chosen. Making himself so important as the future son-in-law to Elliot Jameson.

I wait for the laughter to die down, not to build anticipation but because I'm frantically trying to imagine what other choice I have. Which one I can live with. Dion, who doesn't only want me for my womb but also wants me to study how to please him? To wait on him hand and foot. Dion, who knows he has me in the palm of his hand.

Oh. My. God.

Dion is an Appie. Dion's figured out my dilemma. He knows exactly how many dates I've been on, who my last one was... and figures the cat's in his bag. He might even have found out somehow that I'm tied into the sponsorship of the apartment building. How could he not, with the sponsors introduced and him remembering our date was held in the restaurant of the same building?

And with the way he refuses to drop his steady, almost stalkerish, gaze from mine, I know he's aware. He looks like the cat who swallowed the canary because he knows my exact number of dates.

Paul, who I can't produce because he couldn't run fast enough.

Tom, before Paul, who blocked me from the app before I ever met him in person.

The half dozen before Tom, who I finally ruled out after deciding it was too much work to study other cultures before our date. Those ones had made me decide to go the lazy route and stick to humans.

Brian the liar, who swore he knew other languages.

Or do I admit I've fallen in love with someone who doesn't even want to be picked? Who swore he'd never join the app? Who finally told me he couldn't because he was royalty on his planet?

"Pick me." A profound, riveting voice comes from behind me and curls my insides, just like it used to.

And again, my mind plays tricks on me. Making me think that rumbling, sexy voice is here, right on the stage. But then I notice how the eyes of the audience aren't looking at me any longer, now they're riveted behind me instead.

I whirl around to see Tonnie, in full bodyguard mode, dressed in the black trench coat of their traditional robes. So Matrix-y. But then he steps to the side and my heart pounds in my chest at the sight he reveals.

Khane.

He's wearing an official looking uniform. Something I've never seen before. A prince. He looks like an old-fashioned Prince Charming, even more so than he did at my dad's party. He looks regal and so handsome my heart wants to burst on the spot.

"Khane?" My voice is a throaty whisper, and I'm desperately afraid I've gone off the deep end and made this entire vision up.

"Candace." He moves to me, takes both my hands in his. At the first touch, I know it's real. He's really here. Then he drops down to his knees.

There are gasps from everyone in the audience. No one expected a show like this, because this is ridiculous. He looks like a king, kneeling before a commoner. A nobody. Me.

His sexy baritone rings out, full of authority and sincerity. "I met you through IDA, the app that I fought so hard against and refused to enter. I fell in love with you because of that app. It wove its power even when I thought I was outside its reach."

"Khane?" I whisper again. Maybe those love muffins are still in my system. I blink rapidly to clear the hallucination, but he's still there.

It's too late. This isn't what I agreed to. I promised to allow the app to sort out my mess of a love life. But I don't need it anymore because it's Khane. Yet now I owe on that penthouse suite when Khane is all I want. But here this man is on his knees before me, reaching into his breast pocket.

"I understand from IDA"—he turns toward the audience and winks— "not using my profile, of course, but that of my bodyguard, Tonnie"—there are more chuckles— "that humans propose on one knee and offer a ring to the love of their life."

"I love you too. So much," I admit.

"Candace, my princess, my best friend, crazy female I've always craved... will you marry me?"

Isn't this everything I always wanted? Eff the penthouse.

"Yes, Khane. Yes."

And he finally stands to pull me into his arms. All around us is confused clapping. I can almost hear the thoughts. Does this satisfy the requirements of the app? Technically, he never joined.

Khane pulls back to address the waiting crowd again.

"I know it's not the traditional ending you all expected. You thought Candace should date someone from within the app. But you see, the app brought me to her. I couldn't join, not with my status, but I helped her pick and screen her dates. I consoled her when she kept finding losers more interested in gaining a step up in employment than truly dating. I had unofficial dates with Candace each time, learning about each other, learning about the app, learning about other cultures. We went through everything a couple was supposed to, to learn about each other as the app intended. If not for IDA, I wouldn't be standing here begging for Candace Jameson to forego everything—especially her previous choice—and marry me."

"Is this real? It's me that you want?" I whisper. "Really me?"

"*Inca*, it's always been you. I just needed you to see that. I needed you to experience in that app what I could not simply tell you."

He seals his mouth to mine and I'm barely aware of Dion standing before we come together.

"That's not fair! How can we compete with a prince? That's practically cheating. I lost my first date to him and I'm a paying customer of the app while he never joined!"

I gasp, pulling away. Khane growls, literally growls, a vein popping out on his forehead as his *stremma* emerges in anger at Dion's whine. A beautiful red and white striped man, but oh, the *stremma* is contagious because Tonnie's purple and white stripes emerge too, making them both look otherworldly and exotic.

"My magic spells must really work."

Khane chuckles. "You're utterly crazy. Mad as a hatter."

"Birds of a feather flock together."

"Two peas in a pod," he agrees, nodding his head.

"You're preaching to the choir. Still, I was once bitten but twice shy—"

"—fortune favors the brave," he reminds me.

"Because a trouble shared is a trouble halved. I'm glad we shared everything." I wink. "Including the preparation of the love muffins."

And while the audience may look confused, my dad and Amelia are standing together, grinning broadly. This is assurance that Khane and I are on the same page like no other would ever be with either one of us. No one understands my love language like Khane.

My father speaks up to answer Dion. "It's only because of my app that my precious Candy and Khane met."

There are some chuckles across the room and my father turns to look at us, eying my striped green dress and Khane's bright, red and white *stremma*. "Well, imagine that. We might have to label this latest update the Candy-Khane version. A magical, holiday version of the app that will make everyone rush to try it."

Thunderous applause means sales. Many, many sales. And by the smiles on the sponsors, I think maybe they'll let me slide out of the arrangement with no harm, no foul?

"You'll come home with me and Tonnie?" Khane whispers as my father takes the mic and addresses Dion. "You don't have to worry about the penthouse. We bought both ours and yours. You see, you and I will need one to visit and my bodyguard will need the other to be nearby."

"No offense, but the days of sleeping in the same suite with you two are over." Tonnie rolls his eyes. "I'll protect you from my own place."

Just like that, I'm out of the mess I'd put myself in? I stare at them, bemused.

"*Inca*?" Khane prods.

"Home is where the heart is."

Tonnie scratches his head. "Is that a *yes*?"

"Yes." Khane and I answer together.

Epilogue

Candace:

"Come, little prince. Let me tell you of the greatest love story ever... one about a prince meeting a commoner. The loveliest female in all the land, though odd and quirky. Strange phrases that no one ever heard before would pop out of her mouth."

My little striped son raises his arms for Tonnie to pick him up, which Tonnie does easily, plopping him onto his lap from mine.

"Is that mommy and daddy?" Nitek asks eagerly, his little face that looks so much like Tonnie staring unabashedly at his uncle. "And only daddy knew what she was saying? Like a secret code?"

"Yes. Because he paid an exorbitant amount of money to learn her favorite language and also looked up all those weird sayings. And this story is also about how the strongest, bravest bodyguard of the universe got them together, protected them, and made sure they made the most exquisite prince possible."

Nitek scowls. "The *bravest* prince, Uncle Tonnie. The strongest and the bravest too."

"Ahh, yes. He studies hard and is determined to have a coveted position of bodyguard himself."

"So he can protect the next kid mommy has. And maybe she might be a princess." He leans in to whisper conspiratorially. "I'd like a sweet girl. A delicate little sister. I'd keep her safe and teach her to fight and play..."

My husband—his horns proud and majestic—enters the room with Amelia, Tonnie's pregnant mate. His deep rumbling voice never fails to make butterflies flit in my belly. "Tekki. Are you listening to Uncle Tonnie's tall tales again?"

"Uh, huh." Nitek nods eagerly. "I love them."

Tonnie tickles his side. "Each story is absolutely true, in a manner of speaking, and needs to be retold until they are memorized by receptive little princely imaginations. Treasures for future generations. Now, let me tell you more about the dazzling natural beauty of the bodyguard..."

"And a wicked dragon decided she would keep him." Tonnie makes a chopping motion with his hands. "Because they collect treasures."

"Tonnie Melak'sian. You did not make me a dragon."

Tekki snickers as steam practically rises from Amelia's nostrils.

"Um, no, my love. The dragon's name was *Amelialia* the Wicked."

"The bad dragon wanted the brave bodyguard," Tekki says to her. "'Cause remember, the bodyguard was so han'some, he was dazzling. 'Specially when he smiles, 'cause his teeth are so white an' they match his horns."

"Hmm." Pretty sure Khane snorts, though it's covered up like he's holding back a sneeze when Tekki turns to him.

"Let me guess," Amelia says. "The little prince has to battle his own dragon to protect—"

"Bodyguard," Tekki frowns. "Ima gonna be a bodyguard, Auntie Mel. Trained by the best. Tonnie Chan, a martial arts expert."

"Wasn't that Jackie?" Amelia mouths at me.

I nod, eyes wide. Not sure when Tonnie became a martial arts expert.

"Anyway, the fierce dragon gets *conquered*, literally conquered, by the handsome bodyguard," Tonnie says, pulling Amelia down to the sofa next to him and leaning over for a kiss. He rubs his hand suggestively over her swollen belly and winks, letting her know exactly what he means by the word.

"An' that cute little prince is gonna be protected by the next great and bestest martial arts bodyguard!" Tekki yells, jumping off Tonnie's lap and going into a series of Tai Chi poses on the living room floor. Then he raises one little leg and both his hands to stand in a bird-stance, a fierce little grimace on his features as he tries to snarl. "An' that bodyguard is gonna be Tekki Chan. I can't wait 'til I lose my stripes."

Because a Marjian male carries his stripes until puberty, when they finally disappear only to emerge occasionally with high emotion.

"Well, he needs to eat all his veggies and train first," Khane says amiably, scooping our son off his trembly, one-legged stand and swooping him onto his shoulders.

Tekki giggles and grabs hold of his horns. "Aww, daddy. I only like broccoli."

"You know, not a lot of kids say that," Khane complains. "I blame your mother."

I smile, sure they love my broccoli cupcakes.

"I can't wait 'til Auntie Melia births my charge," he whispers to his father, and then he's so happy he presses a kiss to Khane's ear. It melts my heart.

"Well, poor Auntie Mel has the unfortunate task of birthing the next leader," Khane says. "So, she'll be pregnant a very long time. Three years. Your mommy might have a princess and another prince by then."

"I shall practice my protection duties on my baby sister!" Tekki says. "That's the next one."

"I shall practice making future sons and daughters then," Khane says and with a wicked glint in his eye, leans down to kiss me.

Tonnie snorts and Tekki swoops with laughter as he's swung low enough to kiss me too.

"Well, let's get to the dining hall, shall we? I have a surprise for Uncle Tonnie. Grandpa Elliot is here to talk about his app and Uncle Tonnie gets to sit next to him," Khane says.

Tonnie grimaces and Amelia smooths out the wrinkle on his forehead. It turns out my father brags that he always knew I'd end up with Khane and Tonnie would end up with Amelia and he had to figure out the set up with the two Marjian royals refusing to join IDA. He even claims to have found out that a wine spritzer would knock Tonnie on his ass, thus leading him to chase Amelia while under the influence. Tonnie's heard the story about a million times and if my father has his way, will hear it a million more.

"Grumpa Elliot! Yay! I shall sit on Uncle Tonnie's lap."

Tonnie brightens. "Good idea. You already show great fortitude in bodyguarding," he says, snickering at Khane's eyeroll.

"I wanna call Grumma and Grumpa Melak'sian too!"

"They'll be there," I say softly. "They want to see their favorite sons too."

"An' grandsons," Tekki says, leaning over to rub his Aunt Mel's belly.

This perfect little boy melts my heart. "Did you know the commoner became best friends with the magnificent dragon?" I ask. "Grumpa Elliot matched the dragon to Tonnie Chan with his magical app, you know."

"He did? Grumpa Elliot's app is brilliant!"

This time, Khane and Tonnie both snort.

"I set you up with the commoner long before the app did," Tonnie says.

"Hmm." Khane agrees. "And I introduced you to the dragon long before the app."

But none of us knew Amelia was a shapeshifter—a dragon, to be exact. I think my father knew; he didn't seem surprised when her pregnancy stretched on for so long.

"I bespelled you all with my love muffins," I tell them all. "Without any of you knowing."

"Are we having some with dinner, momma?" Tekki asks.

"Chocolate, my love."

"My favorite! And Prince Amonnie."

I blink, and by the look on Amelia's face, she's just as surprised. "Who?"

"Baby Prince Amonnie. My charge," Tekki explains. "Auntie Amelia and Uncle Tonnie make Baby Amonnie. My cousin. He's still baking too." He eyes Amelia's round belly.

"I like it," Amelia says. "Amonnie."

Tekki nods. "He likes it too. Tole me so."

The four adults don't really know what to say to that.

And later, at dinner surrounded by the rest of our family, when dessert is wheeled out on an enormous gold platter, there's confusion over the cart when the cover is removed to reveal the contents.

It's not the usual chocolate cupcakes.

It's not the love muffins I bake occasionally.

No. This one is a giant pink cake, laced with white bows and ribbons. A gender—and pregnancy—reveal.

"Six months left for that baby sister," I say to my son.

"Yay! Mom," he says, and then the emotion is too much for him. His little eyes fill with tears, just like my dad's, who picks him up from Tonnie's lap to cuddle with him.

Khane pulls me down onto his. "Really, *inca*? Are you sure?"

"We're both pretty sure," I say wryly, rubbing my still-flat belly.

"I love you so much."

When he kisses me, our family breaks out in cheers.

Thank you for reading my story! This sweet and steamy holiday tale is part of the Holidate With An Alien collection, a collaboration of authors telling holiday tales with a science fiction romance twist. Each book is a standalone, containing its own Happily Ever After. They can be read in any order.

I hope everyone enjoyed Khane. If you're in the holiday mood, did you catch *How My Jingleballs Saved Christmas*? It's another collaboration of authors offering you some sweetness for the holidays. Keep reading for a bonus sample.

If you have a moment, I'd appreciate if you would leave a review. It doesn't have to be long, and it doesn't have to be fancy! <u>Anything</u> will do. Reviews encourage me to keep writing.

Feel free to follow on Facebook, Tiktok, or Instagram, or even Bookbub, and sign up for my newsletter to get more up-to-date news, usually sent once or twice a month: https://renamarks.com/newsletter/

And please, keep scrolling to see if you'd be interested in any of my other books. Thank you again!

Other books in the Holidate with an Alien collection:

Skruj—Honey Phillips

Khane—Rena Marks

Yool—Tana Stone

Rixen—Ella Blake

Sleye—Ava Ross

Ozias—Alana Khan

Tinzel—Ella Maven

How My Jingleballs
Saved Christmas

(Sample follows after the blurb)

When your brand-new "kind-of" puppy comes along with his own alien handler.

Tabitha: My best friend gives me her adorable alien puppy. She won't say why, but I suspect her crabby cat, lovingly nicknamed Satanic Sheila by me, wants to eat him.

He's got the face only a mother could love. Poor little scrawny thing—I've named him *Jingleballs*—just shivers and shakes and buries his little face deep into my cleavage to hide.

I have to ignore the strange barking noises that sound more like a man motorboating.

Beloc: Her pet isn't an alien dog—he's my brother.

Punished for a short time to navigate Earth, a species he publicly deemed no better than pets—what better punishment than to become a pet himself trapped in a shapeshifting change?

Except J'ngal finds the most attractive, luscious female on the planet. He has access to her home, her body, her conversations. As a beloved pet, he gets to see her dress, watch her shower, tag along on all her dates. All the things I want to do and can't. So I swear to her I'm his handler from his planet.

Two can play at that game.

———— ❧ ————

114

Other books in this series:

> *How My Krynch Saved Christmas—Sandra R Neeley*
> *How My Alien Saved Christmas—Liz Paffel*

Excerpt from *How My Jingleballs Saved Christmas*:

Tabitha, Planet Earth:

"What the hell is that?"

That is about the size of a cat—a normal cat, not Veronica's mangy Maine Coon, which weighs about the same as Veronica. Her cat, Satanic Sheila, is an evil bitch that I thankfully get to ignore most of the time until Veronica makes me FaceTime with the godawful creature from hell. But this one is small, more like a bony dog, and definitely not of Earth. It's just... shaped weird. Its front legs are shorter than the hind, making me wonder if it tries to walk upright. It's missing ears. But there is a ring of intelligence in the eyes and it is kind of cute too, with its smushed face and itty-bitty nose.

"It's a dog. An alien Chihuahua. You know those aliens that made contact a couple years ago? The Tancieks? One found this little guy had snuck aboard the ship and brought him to the pound."

Oh," I breathe. But I'm stumped. "Why would you take it in?" Everyone in our group knows Veri's a cat girl, not a dog person.

"Well, because it's *alien*," Veronica breathes, like that says it all. "And I didn't realize until afterward that alien dogs and human cats don't get along. Much like human dogs and cats." She shrugs. "But I'm so sad to let my itty-witty bay-beee go!" she sing-songs to the dog. And I swear it preens.

"To be fair, I don't think anything could get along with Satanic Sheila."

"Sheila. It's just Sheila," Veronica says with a frown.

"Maybe if you didn't baby her so much, this cute little thing wouldn't be shivering and given away," I say, bringing the poor scrawny pup to my bosom.

He buries his face in my cleavage.

"Aww," we both sigh. He's so adorable. And terrified by her bully of a cat.

I whisper into his tiny lack of ear. "Did Satanic Sheila scare you?" I ask him. "She's a mean ole beast, isn't she?"

Something emits from the creature's chest. A "grrr" noise. And it's definitely not a bark.

I look up at Veronica. "Are you sure it's a pup?"

She wrinkles her nose. "It does sound like a purr, right? Kind of?"

The puppy raises her head from my cleavage, looks straight at her, and huffs indignantly. It sounds a little bit like a bark. If you stretch your imagination.

"See? Just the way she acts? That's why I think she's a dog. A precious little alien Chi-waaah-waaah," Veronica coos, dragging her words out in baby-talk. "It's all in the attitude. Sheila might be slightly bitchy, the way cats are, but Jingle is, well kind of cocky. Therefore... dog."

"Jingle?"

"Jinglebell. Like Tinkerbell. Which I definitely would have named her if it wasn't Christmas time. But since she came with this cute little collar that has a couple of jingling bells, well..."

I get it. But if Veronica can be wrong about the dog being a cat, she could also be wrong about it being as *she*. I pick it up by the scruff of the neck, making it yelp in surprise, and quickly peer between the little legs.

"Oh!"

The sight that greets me is something I hadn't quite expected. I gulp. The dog has massive balls, pressed together like firm plums, almost the size of his skull.

"What? What is it?" Veronica asks, worried that she's missed something.

Oh, she's missed something. She's definitely missed something. I quickly flash the dog's testicles at her and her jaw drops at the sheer size.

I swear the alien pup has a chuckle at her open-mouthed gape. I put his shivering little body back under my sweater, letting his little head stick out from my neckline.

"Does she have a tumor?" Veronica asks, her lip quivering.

"What? No," I say.

The dog barks at the same time and it sounds strangely like a mimic of my *no*. We both look sideways at it.

"She's a boy," I tell Veri. Then look down at the pup's upturned face. "Going to have to change your name from Jinglebell to Jingleballs," I snicker.

"That's so crass," Veronica huffs.

"What? It's my pet. I can name him whatever I want."

I almost miss the look of satisfaction that crawls over her pretty face. She's got me. She knows I'm stuck with the sweet little guy.

"He's a keeper, right? I knew you couldn't resist. Especially with that *cat allergy* of yours that makes you avoid all of Sheila's important life moments."

For a second my heart races, making Jingleballs twist his little head around to look up at my face because he can feel my heart pounding against my ribs. Does she know I fake my allergy to avoid her beastly pet?

I press a kiss on the top of his scrawny little skull. Satanic Sheila can probably crunch the delicate bone in her maw like a potato chip. "It's dangerous for me to be around cats too," I whisper to the little guy and he rewards me with a short bark. Though it's the oddest sounding bark I've ever heard. Almost as if he says the word *arf*. Strange because I thought he said *no* earlier.

"I'm gonna miss this guy." Veronica leans down to nuzzle Jingle-balls. I hear her whisper into his lack of ear. "Sorry I named you *Jingle-bell*. If it hadn't been Christmas time, I would have called you Tinker-bell. Which is very flattering. Pets everywhere love the name."

I roll my eyes but neither Veronica nor Jingleballs can see it. I don't think there's a dog or cat in the world that appreciates being called Tin-kerbell. Jingleballs, however. Now that's a strong name. Whimsical for Christmas, yet we're able to sneak the word balls in there. The only stronger word is *cajónes*. But Jingle Cajónes doesn't have the same ring.

Jingleballs melts, giving her puppy kisses. So, I step back, making Veronica stand hunched over where I used to be, and glare that I took him away.

I don't need her babying my pup. Jingleballs is going to grow up to be the best, most terrifying watchdog ever. Besides which, he's my pet. And Veronica has already spoiled Satanic Sheila. All of our friends agree.

"Aww!" Sheila protests as I step back. "Promise me you're going to bring him by once in a while to visit! Otherwise, my heart will simply break." She blows a kiss at Jingleballs.

I roll my eyes at her dramatics. "Simply break" my ass. She didn't even know he was a dude, much less a dog versus a cat. Otherwise, she would never have taken him home to Satanic Sheila. Who does that? Who takes a tiny male dog home to an enormous female cat and not expect the bitch to ride him?

"Fine," I snap and her eyes brighten. Come to think of it, Jingleballs brightens too, and that makes me a little jealous. He's my pup, soon to be my vicious watchdog. I can't have her baby him or worse, letting her fat cat pulverize him.

"Supervised visits only. I can't have Satanic Sheila—"

"Just. Sheila," she grits.

"Shee-laa," I drag out, making it sound as though I missed a word in her name. Which I did. The word Satanic, "sit on him. She's heavy. She could break him."

In my bosom, Jingleballs cowers.

"It's not her fault she's heavy!" Veronica protests. "She has thick, long hair. More so than most. It drags her down."

"That and the Puppy Chow you were feeding this poor little guy." Because he certainly looks like he missed a few good bowls to the cat.

Jingleballs burrows face-first into my cleavage, obviously feeling safe and snug in my care. His little tail wags up from the top of my sweater. I reach down and right him so he doesn't suffocate in my ample bosom.

"He's a boob man," Veronica comments. "I wonder if the alien women on his planet don't have boobs?"

"Probably not," I agree. "And he's going to have to get used to being head up anyway. Won't be long before he's too big to be burrowing a tunnel down there."

I swear the dog chuckles.

"Well, I know you're probably going to knit him some adorable outfits since he's so tiny and it's getting so cold," Veri says. "So, I was wondering if maybe you could put together a couple new legwarmers for Sheila? Now that it's December and the snow has arrived—"

"I just made you some a month ago to prepare for the holidays!"

Veri's face turns a little sulky. Not an attractive look at all. "Well, you did! But you didn't bother to come over and measure her—"

"I'm allergic—"

"—and the leggings barely go up her knee. Plus, they're pink. The color makes her look like Petunia Pig, especially when I pair it with her pink cape."

I pause. Barely up her knee? The leggings were measured for my forearm. *My forearm.*

"I mean, it's not because she's curvy," Veri says, flushing a deep red. "It's more like they're too tight because her thighs are so muscular."

I blink rapidly, holding my tongue. I imagine her legs are muscular. They would have to be to hold up the rest of her.

"Umm, sure. I'll work on something bigger."

"Maybe in black?" she suggests. "It's slimming, plus it goes with everything. Should make her pink cape really pop."

"The pink cape that makes her look like a pig?"

"Well, she's hairy so she won't be mistaken for a potbelly," Veri says.

"Hmm." The usual reply I use when she starts bragging about Satanic Sheila because she forgets she just whined that the too-tight pink leggings made her look like a pig.

"Here, look at this latest video."

I grit my teeth. The last few FaceTime calls, I avoided. So now she's going to force me to watch a vid.

I love Veri to death. I do. But I really wish she'd get another point of focus in her life. And seriously, the cat would enjoy being left alone too. She's not a cuddly creature. The grumpy look on her face when she's forced to sit in Veri's lap—

"Isn't she adorable?" Veri's face is glowing, while Jingleballs yelps and buries his face back in my cleavage. I can feel him licking my skin. I tug at him uncomfortably because his tongue tickles.

"Umm, gorgeous," I agree. The cat has a literal frown, her lips turned down as she glares daggers at the camera. In the background, Veri coos about how gorgeous she is and I swear the thing glowers like she knows I'm watching.

"Excuse me." The voice is a deep, bone-tingling, panty-melting, accented baritone. How he snuck up on his without being aware is beyond me because the Tanciek are huge. They all look a little similar too, like genetics are strong within their race. Their females are about six feet, while the males range from six and a half to seven. They're a deep, royal blue color with various sized scales—smaller, petite scale patterns for the women, and larger scales for the men.

Instead of hair, they have some weird protective skull plating, with various wavy or patterned lines. Horns of different shapes, colors, and sizes.

"Hi," Veronica's voice escapes on a breathy sigh. She's an alien buff, even before this race made contact.

"I am Belloc Minosh Kalel of the First House, District Seven of lineage. I'm here—"

"Because I registered Jinglebell!" Veronica announces. "Right here. My paperwork is in my purse—"

"Jingleballs," I correct and the little guy sticks his head out of the top of my sweater, sees the Tanciek, and barks.

In his weird, speaking-way. "Arf. Bow-wow, arf." Those exact words.

But more surprising is when the alien responds. The two carry on a conversation, each one growing louder in volume until it sounds like they're shouting.

"What is going on?" Veronica says.

Everyone stops speaking.

"My apologies. I'm here because—uh, yes, you registered your pet."

From my cleavage, Jingleballs barks.

I swear the alien glares at him. I glare back and protectively place a palm on the front of his body.

"I'm sorry. And you are?" he asks me. His eyes are wide like he just noticed I'm standing here. In fact, he's looking at me in kind the same way Veri is looking at him.

Fascination.

Not that I think he's enamored with me, of course. I'm sure he's curious to see why Jingleballs is nestled in my bra.

"Tabitha Reyes. He's my puppy."

Belloc emits a short laugh. "He's hardly a pup."

I raise my brows.

"Well maybe he is. By the way," the alien chuckles, "I come along with him."

"Excuse me?" This time, Veronica and I squeal together.

He clears his throat. "All... pets of his stature come with a handler. A translator. Until you're able to learn how to care for him."

"For how long?" I ask.

"One of your calendar years, at which point I hand the reins to you."

I narrow my eyes. "How do I know this is real?"

He grins—a shit-eating grin. "Set him down and I'll tell him to approach me, circle my ankles three times and that'll prove to you that I am his handler."

But maybe my little Jingleballs has been trained? So, I counter offer. "I want him to go between your legs and circle one ankle three times. Then he needs to come straight back to me."

Belloc's expression never changes. "Done."

And that seems too easy. "But if he goes to Veronica, or strays anywhere else, that's a deal breaker."

"Set him down." His voice is calm and soothing.

So I take Jingleballs from my sweater, give him a swift kiss on the top of his head because I'm already regretting my ultimatum, I mean, he's just a pup. What if he's curious and goes off to sniff Veronica, who he's used to? Will I have to give him back? Will this alien insist on taking him back to their planet?

Belloc doesn't even kneel down to Jingleballs's level. He stands where he is, barks out a command in his strange alien language and Jingleballs responds.

Belloc turns to me. "He says he'll do one thing extra to prove that I am his guardian. After he returns to you, he'll untie your shoe and then bark for you to let him up." He scowls at Jingleballs. "He's cold. He prefers to be in your sweater."

He looks down at my shivering pup, who's watching his every move.

It's never more apparent that my pup isn't a human dog. He walks on his hind legs, sort of upright, really. In his own way, he trots over to Belloc, goes between his legs to circle one foot three times, and comes back to me. His front paws unties my boot, then looks up at me and gives a short, "Arf."

I stoop down to pick him up and he licks my hands. Then the oddest thing happens. He looks over his shoulder at Belloc as if he's taunting him.

I carefully place him in my sweater and right before he pokes his head down—he sticks his tongue out at Belloc.

"You little shit," Belloc mutters.

Veri and I pass a bewildered look between us. Clearly, there is a relationship between this male and my new puppy.

"So," Belloc says, a wide grin on his face. "Where will we be staying?"

Forced Proximity *Sweet* *V-Card* *Cinnamon Roll* *HEA* *Holiday Read*

Zearn

A mysterious alien planet celebrates their own version of merry holidays. Their wonderful gift-giving idea? Earth ladies as stocking stuffers.

Alyssa: As one of the few female Earthians who works in space, I'm not about to give up my career for marriage and babies. I scorn the idiots who created the podcast "Earth Girls Are Horny." Unfortunately, they've gone viral in a whole new way, calling unwanted attention from galaxies far, far away. The planet Thropian is one secretive and unknown planet who are paying big money to have a bride shipped in a pod to drop down in time for their holiday games. And our horny Earth girls? The volunteers are a mile long, even when it's unknown what the mysterious Thropians look like.

Just not me. No, my job is to test the pod before the actual prize is sent. I'll earn a boatload of money for *not* being a bride.

Zearn: A mate is the last thing on my mind, especially one from a dismal planet who offer themselves to complete strangers as prizes. The utter arrogance is astounding. But when a female lands in the danger zone of our competitive Twelve Days of Cheneca, I'm dispatched as the lead hunter to track her down, and to keep her safe. I do not expect a female who is as much a warrior as me.

A female who is worthy of me. A prize who marries me in the traditional way during the celebrations of our holidays.

With her mouth.

* This book is part of the Stranded With an Alien shared world.

Merry Monsters

Welcome to Wisteria Orchard—where monsters have come out of the woodwork and now live among us.

I would never have thought to move to Wisteria Orchard on my own, but once I'm illegally given a leg up into the protection program, I have to fight hard to rearrange my topsy turvy life. Working in the monster realm gives me a firsthand look at the strongest, the fiercest, and the sexiest monsters out there. Monsters who can protect a girl.

It doesn't take me long to find two of the best. They're unusual best friends, a Gorgon and a Gargoyle. I can't possibly come between them.

Unless it's between the sheets.

Owned By The Orc

I refused marriage, so one was arranged for me, but he's not human. He's orc.

Hannah of the humans: Marriage between an orc and a human is forbidden unless your village needs the protection of their clan, in which case they're willing to sacrifice any maiden who refuses to do their bidding.

Since my father is the lord overseer, I have no choice. I'm to be an orc's arranged bride.

I am Lady Hannah Montierge, despite my title being stripped along with my dignity.

Brun, son of Brachard: One human wormed her way into my heart as children. But she disappeared without a word. When I'm told I must marry a human, I never expected it would be her.

But Hannah pretends she doesn't know me, claiming an illness as a child stole her memories. She wants to believe I'm a savage beast and not the childhood friend who spent hours promising her we'd be together forever.

I'm about to keep that promise. It's her choice as to which.

Other books in the series:

Book 1—**Owned By The Orc**
Book 2—**Saved By The Orc**
Book 3—**Bought By The Orc**
Book 4—**Adored By The Orc**

Saved By The Orc

I owe him. He saved me, even when his kind destroyed my family.

Joanna: When orcs invaded our village, everything changed. The newly self-appointed mayor chose me as his wife—no matter what my choice had been. Living taxes were imposed—if you want to live, you pay.

My new husband pays the tax for both of us, and it keeps me working wage-free in his eatery for my room and board.

But then comes the day when everyone else in our town hides because the orcs return for us.

Latsil: My scars aren't the honorable sort among our people. Mine were forged by capture when my mate sold me to another clan.

I returned home upon her death, broken hearted and in denial that she was one who'd betrayed me. But part of me knows the truth and for that reason, I'll never re-mate. A decision that's challenged when I save a beautiful female from the clan who once imprisoned me. A female who's left her human husband and—like me—is determined never to mate again.

Other books in the series:
Book 1—**Owned By The Orc**
Book 2—**Saved By The Orc**
Book 3—**Bought By The Orc**
Book 4—**Adored By The Orc**

Matched To The Monster

I'm human. He's not.

Lilaina: As the First Daughter of Planet Earth, it's my duty to set an example. When we enter an agreement to re-build the planet, our prized offerings for bargaining are our young, eligible females, starting with me. It's my place to lead by example and I'm only too eager. I can hardly wait to see what handsome, mysterious stranger has been matched for me. Who will sweep me off my feet?

I never expected tentacles.

Juris: The Match Program put together by the Britonian race assures my people that mates from a human planet would be a perfect pair up for us in exchange for our plentiful gold. But those females think of us as monsters. Instead of them allowing us to honor them, they shiver in fear and wish for us to treat them as slaves. They have been taught this way from birth.

On a planet of beautiful, plentiful females repressed by their own males, who are really the monsters?

This is the first book in the Matched Program Series.

The gorgeous species called Britonians had left their planet with a dying sun. They reached an agreement with Earth to clean up our ruined planet with their modern technology in exchange for a new place to live. If it were up to women, we'd allow them to live just to look at them. The Brits are amazing, gold skin, tall and muscular, like avenging angels.

When they hear that most of our men died in the third World War, leaving the sexes vastly mismatched, they offer to begin a Match Program with a distant planet in need of females. It will be completely professional, personality-matching, compatibility, and the possibility of procreation. Plus, the human females will have a guaranteed choice after six months: Remain with your alien mate or come home to Earth.

None of us expected the gorgeous alien species to introduce us to horrifying monsters.

Book 1—Matched To The Monster (Juris & Lilaina)
Book 2—Matched To the Monster Too (Stratek & Tessa)
Also available in a book set!
Book 3—Wanted By The Monster (Jaire & Anya)
Book 4—Wanting The Monster (Relion & Tera)
Also available in a book set!
Book 5—My Monster, My Choice (Elex & Christina)
Book 6—My Matched Monster (Tiran & River)
Book 7—The Monster's Bride (Bronan & Isabel)
Book 8—The Monster's Mate (Skiden & Lucy)

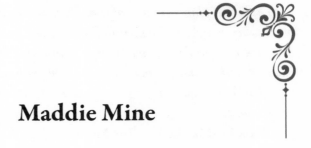

Maddie Mine

She's on the run from a monster. But I'm here to protect her. No one ever expected me to fail.

Maddie had a plan to run away from her ex-husband. She never expected to leave late and have to stay at a small mountain lodge last minute. She didn't expect the owner to be sexy and grumpy—or to shift into a bear right before her eyes. Now that she did see it, though, he isn't going to let her go. But this time, being held captive has a completely different meaning. He's caring and protective and she doesn't want to run. This time, she's found a family.

Until the life she ran from threatens to invade. Can the bears protect her? Or will she pay the price for daring to leave?

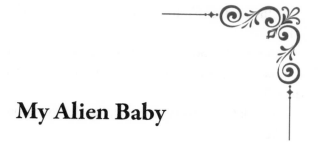

My Alien Baby

Ivory Bellows fell down a well. Ivory Bellows woke up in hell. Better listen to the big blue giant, zip your lip, and hush. Better not stare at his son who makes you blush.

Imagine if you were a giant, fifteen-foot alien from another planet and found a strange being unconscious in a foreign object... a flying pod. The creature is tiny enough to be a child and you'd have such a big heart, you'd want to adopt this poor orphaned child, right?

Only... what if the full-grown human you found didn't know she was your child? What if she thought she was your dinner instead?

The Raza are a people full of honor, faith, and family. Especially Havak of the Jaha clan. His first yun is of his heart, not his blood. But when his mate dies and his beloved yun goes off into the world to study other people and languages, the Creators give him a second chance at life. He happens upon a strange little yun of a species unlike anything he's ever seen.

A strange, five-fingered species.

When the yun wakes and screams, he gives her a bub-bub, wraps her in a pu-pu, and packs her in his sket to bring home.

His huge heart is filled with love for his second adopted yun.

Ivory Bellows wakes up in a strange land filled with blue giants. They threaten her in their strange language, shove a plug in her mouth to keep her quiet and take her home to fatten her up. And marinate her. They must marinate her when she sleeps, because she's swollen and always needs to pee.

Oh, God. She's dinner. It's only a matter of time until they decide when.

But when a hot new alien arrives, the only way she can keep sane is to pretend he's her husband and she's his wife and everything is hunky-dory fine.

Thank God this new arrival, Iik, doesn't know her language.

Yet.

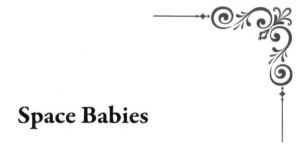

Space Babies

An antiquated ship, rotating through the galaxy of a deserted planet, bears immediate investigation.

Helian Six boards the abandoned vessel to find the long-lost inhabitants in a state of stasis. But the systems are failing, and half a dozen have woken up. The planet below shows long dead bodies, poisoned by the scum of space, a species known as Gorgians.

Strangely, the few who have awakened are much smaller than their planetary predecessors. And not very intelligent. Determined to believe the cute, tiny beings are not pets, the crew of Helian Six decide to train the small warriors to defend the planet. They become the laughingstock of patrol, however, after they commit and realize it will take twenty-two cycles to "rear" the inhabitants.

So they do what any intelligent males would do. Kidnap teachers. And if the females can't manage to avert their eyes from their buff physiques, well, score!

Book 1—Space Babies
Book 2—Baby Soldiers In Space
Book 3—Baby Butterfly Kisses
Book 4—Titi
Book 5—Rock-A-Bye Babies In Space

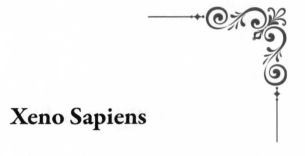

Xeno Sapiens

Catch up with the first novel in the series! The original Xeno Sapiens story.

Futuristic earth finds alien DNA and creates a new species of hybrids in hidden labs. It's up to two small females to teach these beings they're worthy, and beautiful, and loved . . . and to save them from mankind.

My name is Dr. Robyn Saraven. Earth has changed greatly in recent years, the governments of the world merging into one united front, the Global Government. Disease, starvation, and prejudice have been eradicated from our existence, and it appears our growth as spiritual beings is finally on track.

But the discovery of alien DNA pairs a prestigious research facility with our government to create new beings. Suddenly our spiritual growth is halted when mankind plays God. Like old Earth, our modern-day world has to deal with prejudice, corruption, and greed.

Or was it always there, lurking beneath the surface?

Book 1—Xeno Sapiens
Book 2—Earth-Ground
Book 3—Siren
Book 4—Beast's Beauty
Book 5—Almost Human
Book 6—Forbidden Touches
Book 7—Coveting Ava
Book 8—For Everly

Book 9—Assassin's Mate
Book 10—Sextet
Book 11—Tempting Tempest
Book 12—Falling For Trance
Book 13—Damaged Goods
Book 14—Alien's Bride
Book 15—Dual Lives
Book 16—Reson's Lesson
Book 17—A Mate For Max
Book 18—Dragon's Mate
Book 19—Fated

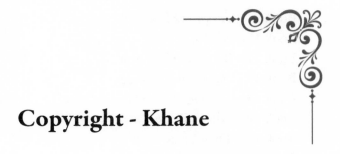

Copyright - Khane

15350676R00087